T0162782

Other books by the author.

LADY ELEANORA

THE DEAD YEARS

TOR'S ODYSSEY

PRETEND
BRIDE

Michael O. Gregory

Order this book online at www.trafford.com
or email orders@trafford.com

Most Trafford titles are also available at major online book retailers.

© Copyright 2020 Michael O. Gregory.
All rights reserved. No part of this publication may be reproduced, stored in a retrieval
system, or transmitted, in any form or by any means, electronic, mechanical, photocopying,
recording, or otherwise, without the written prior permission of the author.

Print information available on the last page.

ISBN: 978-1-4907-9839-4 (sc)
ISBN: 978-1-4907-9838-7 (e)

Because of the dynamic nature of the Internet, any web addresses or links contained in
this book may have changed since publication and may no longer be valid. The views
expressed in this work are solely those of the author and do not necessarily reflect the
views of the publisher, and the publisher hereby disclaims any responsibility for them.

Any people depicted in stock imagery provided by Getty Images are models, and such images are
being used for illustrative purposes only.
Certain stock imagery © Getty Images.

Trafford rev. 11/18/2019

 www.trafford.com

North America & international
toll-free: 1 888 232 4444 (USA & Canada)
fax: 812 355 4082

ABOUT THE AUTHOR

R aised on a ranch in north Texas. Michael entered Military service in 1956. He served two tours in Vietnam. The first with the Airborne Brigade of the 1st Cavalry Division. The second as an infantry heavy weapon adviser on a mobile adviser team (MAT-105). Retired from military service in 1977 as a Sergeant First Class. Michael won the 2009 Beach Book Festival award in the history category for "SHINY BAYONET". A first hand historical account of the first combat operation of the Vietnam war of the men of the 1st Battalion (Airborne), 12th Cavalry Regiment, 1st Cavalry Division (Air Mobile), 10 to 14 October 1965. Michael is the author of several books. He now lives with his wife Jeanne in Evans Georgia.

In memory of Jeanne Oulanoff Blonsky Gregory, my wife of fifty-seven years, who passed away on the 28th of October 2019. May our love endure for all eternity.

ONE

Willliam Hooker sat at the desk, in his father's home office. He had arrived home from Boston five days ago, where he was attending Harvard Collage. He was in his final year of law school. After the Christmas and New Year holiday, he would return to Harvard for a few more classes, some more study, then final exams. Right now, he was catching up on some reading assignments, that would keep him busy through the holidays. William Hooker was a fine-looking man of twenty-one years. He had black hair that he pulled back into a queue, that was tied with a black ribbon. A handsome face, with a strong jaw line and blue eyes, like a calm ocean on a clear day. He stood at five foot eleven inches and weighed one-hundred seventy pounds.

There were many young women in Newport, Rhode Island, where William lived, that would like to catch his attention. However, his heart had already been captured by a young lady by the name of Monique Du Mont; the daughter of Malise and Russine Du Mont, owners of an inn near the city of Reims, France. Monique was now a young woman of eighteen years. They had been corresponding with each other, since William was thirteen and Monique was ten. Their correspondence had started at the suggestion of their parents, as a way to improve their communicative skills in each other's language.

William's father, James, was fluent in French. His mother, Hartene, was born in Quebec Provence of French parents. William grew up speaking French, as well as English. William's father had been a Captain in the Rhode Island Militia during the war for independence from Britain. When the French Army made their headquarters in Providence, Rhode Island, William's father was assigned there as a liaison. That is where he met Monique's father. Ever since the two families had been very close.

William and Monique had just started out as pin pals, however, over the years their relationship had grown to something much more than just friends. Two years ago, they each had had portraits done to send to the other. The portrait that hung on the wall of William's bedroom was of a very attractive young woman, with sapphire-blue eyes and blonde hair, the color of clover honey. Now their relationship had blossomed into an abiding love. Six months ago, William had written Monique proposing marriage.

William's musing was interrupted by the sound of someone coming into the kitchen from the barn. It must be his father coming home from his work at the store. His father was the owner of a general store in Newport. Hearing his mother and father greet each other in the kitchen; William closed the book that he had been reading and stood. He was around from behind the desk when his father entered the room. "Hello, Father. How did it go at the store today?"

"It went well. The weather is cold, but there isn't much snow. People are still out getting those last items for Christmas and New Year."

Reaching into an inside coat pocket, William's father withdrew a letter. "This was delivered to the store today."

"Is it from Monique?" William said, his excitement showing.

William's father gave the letter a whiff and smiled. "It smells like her perfume."

William took the letter, quickly opened it and begin to read.

My dearest William

When I read your last letter, my heart almost leapt out of my breast. I had dreamed of the day that I would read these words from you. Oh, my love, of course I shall marry you. Father and Mother has also agreed to the proxy wedding; although they will also want a traditional wedding in the church before we leave France. It is my most passionate desire to become your wife. You are the only man that I have ever wanted to share my life, or my bed. I shall now go to bed each night in a lonely bed; and dream of the time that I shall feel your body next to me, to feel your lips on mine and to know you in a most intimate way. Please hurry to me, my love.

Your most adoring wife to be
Monique

As he read, his face lit up with a broad grin.

William's father said, "I take it that she gave you an answer to your proposal?"

William looked up from the letter. "Her answer is, yes. She will marry me. She said that her parents have also agreed to the proxy wedding beforehand, so that I can get the necessary documents and passport showing her as my wife before I depart for France, to get her and bring her back here. She also said that her parents would like for us to have a traditional church wedding in Reims, before we leave for America."

William's father nodded. "I can understand that. Although you would already be married in proxy; Monique's family would want to have a traditional wedding in the church."

With a mirthful smile, William said, "I assume that we can expect the same here when I return with Monique?"

William's father laughed, then said, "Why of course. You don't think that we would miss such an event. To get back to what needs be done first, we can get with Pastor Larrimore after church services this coming Sunday, to arrange for the proxy wedding. Now, I need to get ready for dinner. You can continue your studies here."

William nodded. "Yes, Father."

After Church services Sunday, William and his family waited in the vestibule, until Pastor Larrimore finished bidding his congregation farewell. When everyone else had departed, Pastor Larrimore turned to William's father. "What can I help you with, James?"

William's father responded, "Well, George, my son, William has received an answer from Monique, on his proposal of marriage. We now have to make arrangements for the proxy wedding that we spoke of."

Pastor Larrimore thought for a moment. "I'll be very busy through the holidays. What say you, that we have the proxy wedding here at the church at one P M the first Saturday after the new Year?"

William's father offered his right hand. That will be just fine, George. Now, we shall not keep you any longer." They shook hands and departed.

Later on, while the family was seated at the dining room table having lunch, the talk turned to the upcoming proxy wedding. It would be an abbreviated ceremony. There would not be the pomp and pageantry of a formal wedding ceremony. The party involved would just gather in front of the altar, where vows would be exchanged. William's father had just finished explaining how the ceremony would be conducted. He was saying, "Now that you understand, all we will now need is a stand-in for Monique."

Glancing at his oldest sister, William said, "Oh, Father, could Tandra be the stand in for Monique?"

Their father looked at Tandra. "Well, Tandra, would you like to be the stand-in for Monique?"

Tandra thought for a minute, as she played with the food on her plate with her fork. Finally, she said, "Well, Father, If I be the stand-in for Monique during the wedding ceremony; do I get to go to France with William?"

Their father said, "This isn't the time for jest, young lady. You know that you can't go to France now. With the revolution on going, France is just too dangerous a place for you."

Tandra displayed a pout. "That's not fair, boys get to do all the interesting things. At least I had to try. Of course, I will be the stand-in for Monique."

William leaned over to kiss Tandra on the cheek. "Thank you, Tandra."

Tandua replied, "You owe me one, William."

At Christmas the whole family, except for their mother and two servants who were cooking the Christmas meal, attended church services in the morning. The rest of the day was taken up by the Christmas dinner, the exchange of gifts and the visits of friends.

For New Years, William's father hosted a party at their home for some of their friends and business partners. Some of the men brought musical instruments and they had dancing. At midnight, they toasted the New Year of 1793. They then drank a toast to the health of President George Washington.

Finally, the day came, the first Saturday after the new year. Everyone woke-up to fresh snow that had fallen overnight. However, it wasn't such a heavy snow fall that they would have trouble getting to the church. Since the whole family would be going; William's father had decided that both the buggy and gig would be used. William would take the gig with Tandra and Samuel. Father would take the buggy with mother, Clark, Jelline and Ninon.

After a late breakfast, everyone started to get dressed. It being a cold day, everyone wore their warmest wool clothing; the females wearing at least two petticoats for additional warmth. William's father, as usual, wore black for formal occasions. William wore dark-blue breeches and cutaway coat, white shirt with cravat, apricot color waistcoat. Natural color wool hose and boots. Everyone wore heavy wool cloaks with hoods and hats or bonnets. They all wore gloves or mittens. The females also had fur muffs suspended from the neck by a cord, to warm their hands.

While the family had been getting dressed, the servants had hitched up the horses to the buggy and gig. Once everyone was ready; it was but a short trip of under thirty minutes to the Anglican church. Arriving, they found William's older brother Thomas and his wife Virginia, along with other relatives and friends.

Pastor Larrimore was waiting for them: and took charge of the ceremony. He quickly had everyone in their place in front of the altar. Pastor Larrimore, stood with his back to the altar. William and Tandra faced him, with Tandra to William's left side. Everyone else stood to the sides, or to the rear of William and Tandra.

Pastor Larrimore cleared his throat, then said, "Ladies and Gentleman, we are here today to join these two in the bonds of matrimony. William Hooker, Monique Du Mont, are you ready to take your vows?"

Both William and Tandra responded, "Yes."

Pastor Larrimore turned first to Tandra. "Monique Du Mont, will you take William Hooker to be your wedded husband. To have and to hold from this day forward for better, or for worst, for richer, for poorer, in sickness and in health, to love and to cherish till death do you part, according to God's holy law."

Tandra responded, "I will."

Pastor Larrimore then turned to William. "William Hooker, will you take Monique Du Mont as your wedded wife. To have and to hold from this day forward for better, or for worst, for richer, for poorer, in sickness and in health, to love and to cherish till death do you part, according to Gods holy law."

William responded, "I will."

Pastor Larrimore then said, "By the power invested in me, I now pronounce you, William Hooker and Monique Du Mont, husband and wife." With a slight smile, he now said, "We can forego the kissing of the bride."

William and Tandra blushed, as there was a ripple of chuckles through the on-lookers at Pastor Larrimore's wit. Everyone then started to congratulate William, in taking Monique as wife. There would be no reception now. It had been decided that when William returned from France, with Monique, they would have a proper ceremony and reception.

As the other guests departed; Pastor Larrimore took William and his father back to his office, where he filled out and signed the marriage certificate. He then filled out a second certificate. Handing the certificates to William, he said, "Now you send these to Monique. As soon as Monique marries you in proxy, and her pastor signs the marriage certificates; she will send one back to you, so that you can get the passports and travel documents. I included a second certificate so that she would have it to keep under her pillow, until you are there to share her bed."

William and his father laughed. William then took the certificates saying, "I'll get these off to her as soon as I can, with instructions as what to do. Although I would think that her pastor already knows what to do."

The first thing that William did on arriving back home, was to write Monique a letter. He then put the letter and certificates in a packet to be mailed. The first thing Monday morning William took the packet to the post office. Now the hardest part, waiting for the reply began. The next morning, William returned to Harvard Collage, to complete his studies.

Four days later, the packet, inside a mail bag, was put on board a schooner bound for France. Twenty-six days later, the schooner arrived in Nantes, France. There the packet entered the French postal system. It went into another mail bag, that was put on the coach for Paris. Arriving in Paris, the packet was put in another mail bag and put on the coach for Reims.

TWO

Monsieur **Malise Du Mont picked** up the mail and noticed the packet from William, for his daughter, Monique. Right away he knew that this was what she had been expecting and looking in the mail daily for. He didn't have to open it to know what it was. He knew that William and his father would have acted right away to have a proxy wedding; that the packet for Monique contained a certificate of marriage. He would have to visit Father Passy, their parish priest, to make arrangements for a proxy wedding. He was pleased that Monique would be marrying the son of his good friend, James Hooker.

Arriving back at the inn, Malise found Monique in the kitchen with her mother, cleaning up after serving the noon meal in the common room of the inn. Holding out the packet that he had gotten at the post office to Monique, he said, "This came for you; it's from William."

Monique snatched the packet from her father, quickly opened it and started to read the letter.

To My beloved Wife, Monique

> *I was so thrilled at receiving your letter that you had accepted my proposal. It was the most glorious experience of my life, standing before the altar as I gave my most solemn vow to God and all those gathered there, that joined us together as husband and wife. Tandra was the stand-in that said the vows in your name. So, my wife, complete the ceremony quickly and send me a copy of the*

certificate, so that I may obtain the necessary documents, then come for you. Take care until we are together.

Your loving husband,
William

Monique put the letter to her breast. At last, William was her husband. Soon she would take her wedding vows and become his wife. Then by this coming summer, he will be here to take her with him to America. Over the years, during their correspondence, William had told her quite a lot about the United States and Newport, Rhode Island. She was sure that she would love it there.

Her father interrupted her musing. "Monique, you can let me have the marriage certificates for now. I shall pay a visit to Father Passy and make arrangements for the wedding ceremony."

Handing the marriage certificates to her father, Monique said, "Yes, Father, and please ask him to make it as soon as possible."

The next day, Monique's father spoke with Father Passy after morning mass. Father Passy consulted his schedule, then gave Monique's father an open date when he could perform the proxy wedding ceremony. Monique's father thanked Father Passy and left for home.

Back at the inn, he found Monique getting ready to serve lunch to their patrons in the common room. Seeing him, she said, "Well, Father, what did Father Passy have to say?"

Her father smiled at her, "He gave us a date. It will not be this coming Saturday, but the following Saturday. He will perform the Wedding ceremony after the morning mass."

Monique let out a squeal and clapped her hands in front of her face, as she exclaimed, "Oh, that's wonderful! Then in ten days, I shall be Madame Hooker. I have been making a new gown to wear for the wedding. It is almost done. It will be ready in plenty of time."

Her father embraced her and kissed her on the forehead. "That's fine, Monique. I'm sure that in your wedding gown, you will be the most beautiful woman in Reims."

Monique gave her father a broad grin. "Oh, Father, you flatter me so much."

Her father gave her another kiss, this time on the cheek. "It is no flattery. You are the sweetest and most gracious daughter a man could have." He then released her. "Let us go and take care of our guests."

It was about two in the afternoon. A young woman, carrying a travel bag, approached the outskirts of a small hamlet about twelve kilometers south-east of Versailles. She turned into the first street to the right as she entered the hamlet, stopped at the forth house on the right, that belonged to, Madame Jackquel Gauzet and knocked on the door. It was a typical three-room house owned by the working class in France. A central room used for dining and other family functions, with a bedroom on each side. A kitchen had been built onto the back of the house, with a root cellar to the side. There was a well about ten meters to the rear of the house.

When Madame Gauzet opened the door, the young woman said, "Hello, Mother."

Madame Gauzet embraced her daughter. "Oh, Azura, it's so good to see you." Madame Gauzet took her daughter's bag. You must be weary from the road. Come in and have a seat. I'll put your bag in your room. Then make some coffee."

Azura was the youngest of Madame Gauzet's four daughters. The first three were of her husband. Azura was born four years after the death of her husband. Azura's father happened to be a soldier that was there when her mother felt a need for someone to comfort her. By the time she realized that she was pregnant, she couldn't even remember the father's name. Azura's name was due to a legacy from her father. She had blue eyes, almost the color of a clear blue sky as reflected through ice. To this was added fine light-blonde hair like corn silk. This made for a most striking appearance.

Handing over her travel bag, Azura said, "It wasn't so bad on the road. The weather is cool, not really cold. It was a pleasant walk."

Madame Gauzet put her daughter's travel bag in Azura's bedroom, as Azura took a seat at the dining table. After putting a pan of water on the stove for coffee, Azura's mother joined her at the dining table.

Looking at her daughter, Madame Gauzet said, "I'm glad to have you home, but I wasn't expecting you. Had there been any changes?"

Azura nodded. "Yes, you can say that there are changes at Versailles. Every one of prominence at Versailles is either in exile, in hiding, or in prison; that includes my mistress, Madame Du Barry. There was no point in staying anymore."

Madame Gauzet reached out and patted the back of her daughter's hand. "I'm glad that you are back home. I have been afraid for you in Versailles. There have been rumors of people that associated with or worked for the nobility being arrested."

Azura reached out and squeezed her mother's forearm. "Don't worry, Mother. I'm back home to stay now. I just plan to stay in or around the house and not draw attention to myself."

Azura's mother looked into the kitchen, then went to make the coffee.

The next ten days for Monique seemed at times to fly by; then at other times craw along. She continued with her duties at the family run inn of helping her mother in the kitchen, serving in the common room and milking their two cows every morning and evening. In between her duties, with her mother's help, she managed to finish her wedding gown.

The day before the wedding ceremony, Monique went to confession. Father Passy sometimes wondered why Monique even bothered at times to come to confession. Some of the young women in the parish had some rather interesting sins to confess. On the other hand, it seemed that at times Monique had to think hard to come up with a few minor sins, so that she would have a reason to come to confession. She had to be the most chaste young woman he had ever known.

Finally, the day of her marriage arrived. The whole family dressed in their best for the wedding ceremony. Monique's older brother Percival would be the stand in for the groom. He looked so dashing dressed in his National Guard uniform of white shirt, white cravat, white waistcoat, breeches, hose and blue uniform coat. Even her father was wearing his old uniform, that he had worn during the war for American Independence from Britain. Monique dressed in her wedding gown. Her father had been generous and she had been able to find a very lovely lavender silk brocade to make her wedding gown. Everyone had to agree that they had never seen her more beautiful. In her hair she wore a comb of silver and mother of pearl, covered by a white-lace scarf. When all the family was ready, they departed for the church.

After everyone that had attended the morning mass had departed. The wedding party gathered in front of the altar. With his back to the altar, Father Passy had Monique and her brother Percival stand facing him, with Monique to the left of her brother. The rest of the wedding party gathered around Monique and her brother.

When he seen that everyone was ready, Father Passy said. We are here to join Monique Du Mont and William Hooker in the bonds of holy matrimony. Who gives this woman to be married to this man?"

Monique's father said, "I do."

Father Passy then spoke to Monique. "Monique Du Mont will you take William Hooker to be your wedded husband. To have and to hold from this day forward for better, or for worst, for richer, for poorer, in sickness and in health, to love and to cherish, till death do you part, according to God's holy law."

Monique responded, "I will."

Father Passy then turned to Monique's brother. "William Hooker, will you take Monique Du Mont to be your wedded wife. To have and to hold from this day forward for better, or for worst, for richer, for poorer, in sickness and in health, to love and to cherish, till death do you part, according to God's holy law."

Monique's brother responded, "I will."

Father Passy then said, "I now pronounce William Hooker and Monique Du Mont Hooker husband and wife."

The ceremony was over. Everyone started to congratulate Monique and wish her a happy and fruitful marriage. She was really thrilled when one of her friends addressed her as Madame Hooker for the first time.

Back home at the inn, they had a reception with family and a few friends for Monique. It was just a mid-day meal where everyone could show their respects to the bride. Monique's parents planned to have a proper reception when William arrived, and they were married in the church.

Sunday evening Monique was serving in the common room. They had a big crowd for the evening meal. Monique was serving dinner to a man of about thirty years, thereabouts. He was an average looking man that few people would take a second look at, or remember. However, the one thing that Monique noticed when she took his order, was how he had appraised her with his eyes.

When she had returned to the table with his dinner, he had tried to take her hand, but she was fast enough to pull it away. He then said, "Well, Mademoiselle, you're a comely young woman. What say that we have a good time this evening?"

Monique gave him a baneful look. "It is Madame, Monsieur, not Mademoiselle. I can assure you that my husband would not be pleased." She turned on her heal and walked away. This is something that she had had to deal with ever since she had entered puberty. Now she had her new married status to wave in their faces. She now had a copy of the marriage certificate that she kept on the night table next to her bed.

The next day Monique's father mailed the other marriage certificate, addressed to William's father in Newport Rhode Island. The letter went into a mail bag that was put on the coach for Paris. At the Paris post office, it was put into another bag that was put on the coach for Nantes. At the Nantes post office, it was put into another bag and put aboard an American schooner bound for Boston. At the Boston post office, the letter was put in another bag and placed on another ship bound for Newport, Rhode Island.

THREE

William Hooker returned to Harvard Collage to complete his required classes, then take his final exams. By early March he had completed all his requirements, passed his final exams and received his diploma. Now he was free to return home to Newport, Rhode Island and start to build his future.

Going to the Boston Harbor Masters office, he found that a small trading schooner was leaving for Newport on the morning tide. He was able to book passage for a small fee. It would just be a short sail around cape Cod, Nantucket, then on to Newport. They would be there the following day.

The next morning William departed Boston aboard the schooner James Dunn. At this time of year, it was still cold off the coast of New England. However, the weather was good, and expected to hold on their passage to Newport.

The next day, about thirty minutes past the noon hour, the schooner James Dunn tied up to the pier at Newport, Rhode Island. As soon as the gang plank was made secure, William departed with all his baggage. Being that he would not be returning to Harvard. He had brought everything that he had accumulated with him. His father's store was but a short distance from the pier. William hired two stevedores to help him carry his luggage to his father's store. Arriving at the store, he was greeted by his father and older brother, Thomas.

His father embraced him, saying, "Welcome home, William. We are all proud of you for what you have accomplished."

William embracing his father in turn, said, "Thank you, Father. It was a long time, but it is behind me now. I shall go see Alexander Jessup tomorrow. He said that when I graduated from law school, he would take me in to his practice as an associate."

His father patted him on the shoulder. "You have made a good choice, becoming an associate. By the time that you have the experience to take over the practice, Alex will be ready to retire and want to sell his interest in the practice."

William and his father now broke their embrace. His Brother, Thomas stepped up and shook his hand. "Welcome home, William."

"Thank you, Thomas." William replied.

William's father now said, "Now, William, why don't you just run along home. I'm sure that your mother is anxious to see you. I shall have a wagon take your baggage home for you.

Without further words, William left the store and headed home.

Arriving at home, William went directly to the kitchen. As soon as he came through the door, his mother embraced and kissed him on the cheek. "Oh, William. it's so good to have you back home to stay. I have fresh linens on the bed; your bedroom is ready for you. Would you like something to eat or drink?"

Breaking the embrace and sitting down at the kitchen table, he said, "I would like to have a cup of hot tea with milk and sugar."

William's mother turned to make the tea for him. When the tea is ready, she had a seat across the kitchen table from William. As William started to drink the tea, his mother said, "I assume that you will be seeing Alex Jessup soon."

William nodded. "Yes, I plan to see him tomorrow. I'm anxious to get my law practice going."

His mother said, "That's good, William. There is, however, something that your father has been eager to show you. I would assume that he would like to show it to you tomorrow."

William took another sip of tea, then set his cup down on the table. "Well, if Father has something to show me tomorrow, I can delay going to meet Alex Jessup."

William and his mother talked a little more, as William finished his tea. He then went up to his bedroom to get settled back in. Everything was as he had left it. He stood looking at the portrait of

Monique. He enjoyed looking at her. Soon it wouldn't be just oil paints on canvas, but Monique in person. He yearned for that day.

That evening at dinner William was kept busy with his siblings' questions. Samuel, at fourteen, was already thinking about collage. He had a lot of questions for his brother about Harvard. William told him about Harvard Collage. William also told his brother that there was to be a collage opening soon in Provence, Rhode Island. The name of this new collage was to be Brown. It would be a lot closer to home for Samuel that Harvard.

William's sister, Tandra ask him if the ladies of Boston were wearing any new fashion. William had to admit that he knew little about women's fashion. That when he looked at a girl, all he looked for was if she was gorgeous; and rather or not she was smiling at him. Everyone at the table got a good laugh at the frown that Tandra gave her brother. William's father then told him that he would like to show him something in the morning, before he went to Alexander Jessup's office.

The next morning, after breakfast, William's father hitched up one of their horses to the gig. He and William then left Newport by the north road. About two and a half miles from town they came to a house and barn. It was a large house, with an even larger barn. Although it had been neglected of late, everyone could see that it had once been a grand home.

They pulled off the road, onto the drive, in front of the house. They dismounted from the gig; then William's father led him to the front door of the house. William's father opened the door and they went inside. They stood in a wide hall that ran from the front door to a stair case at the back of the house. There were two rooms on each side of the hall. Looking from the front door to the stair case, the room at the left rear would be the dining room. The kitchen was built onto the left rear of the house, from the corner of the house to the stair case. At the back of the house, on the other side from the kitchen, was the entrance to a large root cellar.

William's father started to show him the house. There were the same layout of rooms and hall on the upper floor. There were bulk items in some of the rooms to be sold in his father's store. The previous owner left most of the furniture, that was now stored in the upper rooms. William recalled that it was one of the properties that his father purchased from Tory's toward the end of the war. He had paid much less than the properties were worth. In most cases, the property of Tory's was abandoned, when they fled at the end of the war. Of the properties that his father had been interested in, he wanted a clear deed that no one could challenge. He ended up giving them just enough to get a start somewhere else.

When they finished inspecting the house, they went to the barn. Along with the large open space at the front of the barn, there were two milking stalls, four stalls for horses, tack room, feed room, tool room and a large hay loft. Adjacent to the barn, was a small cottage for domestic help to live in. There was also an old gig with faded blue paint in the barn Next to the barn and behind the house was what was left of the garden and orchard.

William's father said, "William, this house and barn sits on fifty-seven acres. What do you think of it?"

William knew the property well enough. Of all the properties that his father had purchased from the Tory's, this was the one he liked the best. Looking around, William responded, "It needs some work, but it is a splendid place."

Taking a document from his inside coat pocket, William's father said, "I have deeded it to you. You now have a home to bring Monique back to. I shall have all my goods moved out. The furniture left by the previous owner will be yours. I will even hire some men to help you get the place cleaned up. Mostly it just needs a fresh coat of paint to be made whole again.

William embraced his father. "Thank you, Father, Monique and I will fill it with your grandchildren."

His father stepped back, then handed William the deed. "Your mother and I would enjoy that. Now, let us be going. I'm sure that Alex Jessup is eager to put you to work."

Arriving at the law office Alexander Jessup, William and his father noticed a new sign hanging in front of the office. The new sign read, Jessup and Hooker Esq. Attorneys at Law. William was thrilled to see his name on the sign.

Entering the office, they found Alex Jessup waiting for them. He showed William his desk, then took out a bottle of bourbon whiskey and three glasses. They then drank a toast to the new partnership.

After the toast, William's father left for the store.

William went to his desk. Alex then started to bring him up to date on the actions that they were handling. William had had many talks with Alex about the practice over the last year. Newport being a sea port, cargoes were always moving in and out of the port. There were always contracts to be drawn up. There were Wills to be drawn up. Sales agreements for real estate and other properties. There was also the occasional criminal case. There was more than enough work to keep the both of them busy. Alex started out giving William work that he could easily handle. Alex would give him something harder when he felt that William had the experience to handle it.

William was joyful to be finally be doing the work that he loved. Between his work at the office and working on his new house when he had the time, there wasn't much time for anything else.

Three days before the end of April a schooner made port at Newport, Rhode Island. It had sailed from Boston the day before. It dropped off the mail bag for the post master. The post master sorted the mail. There was a letter from France for James Hooker. Seeing who the letter was from. The post master hand delivered it to James Hooker at his store. Seeing that the letter was from Monique's father, James promptly left his son, Thomas to mind the store and headed for William's office.

Arriving at William's office, his father handed the letter over to his son. Opening the letter, William found the completed marriage certificate. With a big grin on his face, William exclaimed, "At last! Now I can go to get Monique!"

After breakfast, Azura's mother had gone to the bakery for bread, while her mother was gone, Azura gathered dead branches from the woods for fire wood for the kitchen stove; and cut fodder for the rabbits. She was sitting at the table when her mother returned from the bakery. One look at her mother's face and she knew that there was bad news. "What's wrong, Mother?"

Her mother dropped her shopping on the table and had a seat across from Azura. She took a couple of deep breaths, then said, "Bad news, Napier Boyer was arrested on charges of being a royalist sympathizer. The people at the inn tried to warn him when the agents from the Committee for Public Safety came looking for him. They were at the house before he could get away."

That brought to the fore Azura's fear that someone would denounce her as a royalist sympathizer. Before she could say anything, her mother continued, "We need to start making plans now. So that if they come after you, you are not caught unawares. I have already gone by the inn to ask them to give warning if anyone comes looking for you. Now, even with a warning we would have no more than a few minutes for you to get away."

Azura's mother now got up and went into her bedroom. When she returned, she had a long belt made of heavy linen. It was made in such a way as to have several pockets covered over with a flap of cloth. There were long ties so that it could be wrapped around the waist and tied. Having seen one before, Azura knew it to be a money belt. Taking the belt and a candle, her mother lit the candle and led Azura down to the root cellar. There her mother removed a lose stone from the wall of the root cellar. Behind the stone was a cavity. Within the cavity was a leather pouch. Her mother removed the pouch. It made a clinking sound from all the coins it contained. Her mother counted out some coins, both gold and silver, then put the leather pouch back in the cavity and replaced the stone. She then took Azura into the house and sat again at the table.

When her mother had put all the coins into the pockets of the belt, she said, "Azura, stand up and raise your skirt and petticoats over your waist. Azura did as her mother requested. Her mother tied the belt securely about her waist. "Okay, Azura, you may let your skirt and petticoats down now."

Once Azura had her clothing back in place, her mother continued, "Now, Azura, you will wear that money belt always. Never take it off for any reason. You will even sleep with it at night. This was to be your dowry. If you must flee, you will need it to start a new life in England. What you must do is pack your travel bag. Do not pack so much that you can't carry it for some distance. You will keep it in the storage shed. Make sure that you have sturdy shoes that you can walk in in your travel bag. Every night when you go to bed, you will have all of your clothes in a bundle on top of your night table, so that you can just grab it and run. If we get a warning in the middle of the night that they are coming for you, don't even take the time to dress. Just grab your bundle of clothing and run. Go out the back way. Grab your travel bag as you pass the storage shed. Keep on going out the back gate. Keep going until you are at least two-hundred meters into the woods. You can then stop long enough to dress. Then get far away and head for Paris. There, if you can get travel documents, get to a port and take a ship to England. Do you understand?"

Azura nodded. "Yes, Mother, I understand."

FOUR

William took the next ship out of Newport, Rhode Island bound for Boston, arriving the next day. Departing the ship, he went straight for the government office that provided passports and travel documents. After presenting the proper documents and paying the fees, he was told to return in three days to pick up his documents.

Leaving the passport office, William went to a house convenient to the Harvard campus that was owned by an elderly couple, Lawrence and Purity Cooper, whose children were grown and on their own. They earned extra income by renting rooms to people that were visiting Harvard. He was well known to them and was able to get a room in their home while he was in Boston.

After securing a room at the cooper's house. William visited with some of his friends at Harvard. His professors were interested in hearing about how he was doing with Alexander Jessup. William told them that he liked working with Alex; and that when Alex retired, the practice would be his.

For the remainder of his stay in Boston, William enjoyed visiting places that were so familiar to him. He knew the better taverns, where the ale, food and fellowship were excellent. On the last day before he picked up the documents, William went shopping at a jewelry store. There he purchased two plain-gold bands. He was easily able to get one that fit his ring finger well. As for the second ring, he ended up having to describe Monique's approximate size, weight and rather she had a delicate or more robust build. The jeweler ending up selling him a ring that he said, should be a close fit for Monique. If not, it could easily be resized.

The next morning William picked up the documents at the passport office. He was able to find a ship that was sailing for Newport that same day. After an overnight trip, he arrived back at Newport the afternoon of the next day.

The next few days were busy for William, getting ready to leave for France. For William, the hardest part of preparing for the trip was packing his bag. He had been off to Collage for a few years, but had never made a trip such as this. Finally, his mother had him put everything that he wanted to take with him on the bed. She then had him put away over half of it. They ended up with two cutaway coats, one indigo-blue and one charcoal-gray. There were three pair of breeches, One indigo-blue and two slate-gray. There were three waistcoats of cornflower-blue, plumb and pine-green. With this his mother let him put enough shirts, cravats, underwear and hose to get by with. The weather being mild in France this time of year, he only needed one pair of shoes that he would wear and a Black light-weight cloak.

When his mother had finished. He could easily carry everything in one bag. On the day of departure, one change of clothing from the travel bag would be worn; and his razor, with soap cup and brush would be added.

Three days later William had a ship that would take him to Nantes, France. It was the schooner, Zealous Maiden. It would be sailing on the morning tide in four days. It was one of the ships that William's father was part owner of. William's cousin, Frank Cooper was first mate. The Captain was John Mercer.

The Evening before William's departure, the family had a departure party for William. His mother baked a ham with honey apples and raisins, served it with baked sweet potatoes, corn on the cob and other side dishes. Dessert was egg custard. Members of the family gave William small gifts to give to Monique's family.

William's father had a going away gift for his son. He made a show of presenting it to him. It was even wrapped in bright green tissue paper. Even with all that, its shape couldn't be concealed. William knew that it was a walking cane. As he tore the wrapping paper away, he knew he had seen the cane many times. It had been one in a shipment of canes that his father had gotten for the store. The other canes sold well. However, this cane was a little different. The black lacquered shaft was of hickory a little larger in diameter that most walking canes. The butt of the cane was clad in brass, with a large brass ball about the size of a plumb on the end. The tip of the cane was also shod in brass. Being heavier than most canes, it had not sold. His father, being a Yankee merchant, had found a use for it. Holding up the cane, William said, "Thank you, Father, it is just what I wanted. With my new top hat, I shall at least look the gentleman."

His father said, "I knew that you didn't have a cane; and a gentleman should have a good cane. Now you shall look your best in Paris."

After all the gifts were taken care of, they just sat around and talked until it was time for bed.

The next morning everyone had breakfast. After breakfast, everyone who had no pressing business elsewhere, went to the dock with William to see him off. William went on board and put away his travel bag. He then stood at the rail and chatted with his family, who stood on the pier, until the tide turned. The mooring lines were cast off and taken aboard. William waved a last farewell to his family, then they were moving to the open ocean.

Monique woke up to the knock at her door. She heard her mother's voice on the other side of the door. "Monique, it's time to get up."

Swinging her legs from beneath the bed covers and over the edge of the bed, Monique responded, "I'm up, Mother."

Monique dressed quickly, then went to the kitchen. Her mother already had the bread sliced and was now making the coffee. The coffee was made in a large kettle. First water was brought to a boil; then the coffee grounds were dumped in. once the coffee grounds settled to the bottom of the kettle, the coffee was ladled out of the kettle into pitchers. Milk and sugar were then added. Monique put the bread and butter out on the tables. She then put out strawberry preserves and brie. People complained about the coffee now. With France being cut off from her overseas colonies, cane sugar was unavailable. There was only beet sugar, if you could get it.

After breakfast it was time for Monique to milk the cows. She got the buckets and went out to the barn to milk the cows. Due to the lengthening days of the season, as it advanced towards summer, Monique no longer had to take a lantern with her, to do the morning milking. There was now enough light in the barn to see well without a lantern.

Unawares to Monique, during the night a stallion belonging to one of the inns guests had caught the scent of a mare in heat. In his excitement, he had kicked the sides of his stall. A piece of board was knocked loose to fall into some soiled straw from the stalls, with the point of a nail sticking up.

Monique completed the milking without any difficulty. She then picked up two pails of milk and started back to the kitchen. She had taken little more than a dozen steps when her foot came down on the point of that exposed nail. The nail penetrated the sole of her shoe, went all the way through her foot and out the top of her shoe. With a cry of pain, she jerked her injured foot off the ground, became over balanced and fell. The milk that she had been carrying spilled and sloshed all over her and the barn floor. Crying out in pain, Monique was able to extract the nail from her foot.

Monique's mother was startled to see Monique come limping in from the barn all wet, dirty, disheveled and crying in pain. Her mother exclaimed, "What happened, Monique!"

Falling into a chair, Monique said, "I was bringing the milk in, when I stepped on a nail."

Her mother looked and saw a little blood on her shoe. Removing the shoe and bloody hose, Monique's mother inspected the wound. She could see that it was a puncture wound that went all the way through the foot. Taking a shallow basin of hot water, clean rag and soap, her mother cleaned the wound the best that she could. She then bandaged the foot with clean strips of linen.

When she was done, her mother said, "Well, Monique, you will not be able to work the common room for a few days, you can help me here in the kitchen."

Monique nodded. "Yes, Mother."

Her mother then said, "Can you get to your room on your own to change. Or do you need help?"

Starting to stand, Monique said, "I can make it on my own, Mother."

All that day, Monique helped her mother in the kitchen. She prepared vegetables and did any other thing that could be done while sitting at the table. By that Evening Monique had a pounding headache and took to her bed. The next morning Monique had developed a stiffness in her neck and jaw; and then the muscle spasms started. They were first in the jaw, then other parts of the body.

Monique's parents became alarmed and sent for a physician. The Doctor examined Monique and delivered his diagnosis, that was tantamount to a death sentence. Monique had tetanus. Hearing this, Monique's mother broke down into tears. Her father remained stoic, trying his best to be the rock that the family would need to lean on.

As Monique's illness progressed, her whole body became rigid. She would have muscle spasms that were strong enough to tear muscles and break bones. The rigid muscles in the face gave her the appearance that she was grinning. From time to time she would make gasping or grunting sounds as she struggled to breathe.

All through her ordeal, Monique's mother or father was at her side. They tried to make her as comfortable as they could, although they wondered that she was even aware of it. Even so, her parents hoped that at some level she was still aware that they loved her.

At noon of the fifth day, Monique's parents called for Father Passy. Father Passy was aware of Monique's illness and had been expecting the call. Arriving at the inn, Father Passy was escorted to Monique's bedside. Seeing for himself that the end was near, Father Passy gave the last rites to Monique. Father Passy looked at giving the last rites to someone who was at the end of a long life wasn't so hard. It was just the last act in a long life for a person. However, having to give last rites to someone like Monique was especially hard.

The next morning, about an hour before sunrise, Monique breathed her last. At the end she had the marriage certificate under her arms, next to her heart. The portrait of her husband, William Hooker, whom she would never see in this lifetime, hung on the wall over her bed.

Her father had a mortician prepare the body for interment. For burial she was dressed in her wedding gown, with the comb and lace veil for her hair. Her hands were clutching her rosary over her heart, with the marriage certificate tucked in underneath. Her face was heavily made up to hide the bruising inflicted by the illness.

After the funeral, Monique's father wrote a letter to William's father, letting him know of Monique's death. He told him how she had come down with tetanus and died. The next morning, he went to the post office to mail the letter. As he left the post office, he hoped that the letter reached its destination before William left for France.

FIVE

The schooner, **Zealous Maiden, docked** at Nantes, France. William Hooker was already on the main deck with his travel bag, waiting for them to run out and secure the gangplank. This was the first time that William had been outside of North America; Canada being the only foreign country that he had ever visited. Everything here seemed so exotic. He thought that there could even be houses here in Nantes older than the first colony of James Town. At least he spoke the language fluently.

As soon as the gangplank was run out and secured; William picked up his travel bag and left the ship. There were officials ashore that checked his passport and travel documents; then directed him to an inn where he could catch the coach to Paris. It wasn't a long walk and he was soon there. There he was told that a coach would be leaving for Angers, the first leg in the journey to Paris. William reserved a seat in the coach, then went to the common room of the inn to have dinner and wait for the coach.

Three hours later the coach arrived on time and William boarded. He found that he would have company on the coach to Angers. There was an elderly couple returning to Le Mans, after visiting their daughter and son-in-law, following the birth of their first child, a son. There was also a wine merchant, returning to Poitiers.

The elderly couple were very excited about the birth of their grandson. They already had three granddaughters, but this was their first grandson. After three girls in a roll, they had begun to wonder if they were destined to have a grandson.

The other person in the coach, the wine merchant, had been in Nantes to arrange the sale of wine to exporters. William was polite, but didn't find much interest in the wine exporting business. When the other passengers found out that William was American, the topic of conversation turned to the revolution. William was asked his opinion on the revolution. William had to admit that with all his studies at Harvard Law School, there wasn't much time to follow the revolution in the newspapers.

William was then asked how they had done it in America. He explained to them that after gaining their independence, they had tried to govern the nation through the articles of confederation, that wasn't working too well. Then six years ago they had a convention and wrote the constitution to form a federal government. The people then elected General George Washington as our President.

At Poitiers William changed coaches for Tours. His fellow passengers were a young couple that preferred to keep their own company. That was alright with William. He spent his time reading, or watching the scenery roll by. The only thing that annoyed him was the occasional barricade, what the French called a road block set up by the Committee of Public Safety, where everyone's papers were checked. William never had any trouble with his papers. As soon as the committeemen saw the stamps and seals of the United States of America on his documents, they passed him on. He soon came to understand that the barricades were frequently moved, so that no one could be sure of where they would be.

At Tours, William took a room at the inn to get some rest, before traveling on to Paris. After a night's sleep, William continued on to Paris. For the rest of the trip to Paris, William's companions in the coach were a French Army colonel and his aid, a young lieutenant. The colonel was interested when William told him that his father had been a captain in the Rhode Island Militia during the American War for Independence. William found out that before the French Revolution, the colonel had been a First Sergeant of an infantry company. Now he was a colonel in command of an infantry regiment. One other thing that William learned from the colonel, was that you could sometimes find better lodging accommodations than the local inns by asking the coachman.

When the coach arrived in Paris, William had decided to take a room overnight, so that he would be fresh when he arrived in Reims. He asked the coachman and was directed to a house not far from the inn where the coach made its stops. The house belonged to Monsieur Foutayne Minot and his wife, Odetta. They rented out room by the day or the week. They even had a very nice room in a converted carriage house. They charged extra if you wanted to take your meals with them. William took the room in the carriage house and paid extra for the meals.

At dinner that evening William entertained his hosts with the tale of how he and Monique had fallen in love through their correspondence, of how they had married by proxy and that now he was here in France to bring Monique back to America with him. They saw it as a most interesting love story. William, being an American, they wanted to know about the American Revolution. They told William that the French people took inspiration from the Americans, that a people could throw off the bonds of a tyrant and take control of their own destiny. Monsieur and Madame Minot were in favor of the idea of liberty and equality, but being devout Catholics, they didn't like how the church was being persecuted by some factions within the Committee for public Safety.

The next morning William returned to the inn to take the coach to Reims. Some of the German States were moving to invade France after the atrocities committed on the French Royal family by the revolutionaries. His fellow passengers were French Army officers returning to their regiments near the German frontier.

There were the usual questions about where he was from, where he was going to and why. They seemed to like the story about him and Monique. There were also the usual questions about the United States and the War for Independence from Britain.

From Paris to Reims was about one-hundred miles. By the evening of the first day there was little talking in the coach. Everyone was getting tired and just wanted to rest. The coach kept going all through the day, the night into the next day, with occasional stops to give the passengers a short break, or to change horses and drivers. The coach arrived in Reims just after noon of the second day.

Leaving the coach, William hired a buggy to take him out to Monique's parents inn. As soon as he walked through the door of the inn, Monique's father recognized him as James Hooker's son, William. He then knew that the letter hadn't arrived in time. He would have to break the news to William. But first he would have to get William out of the common room, to some place more private.

Monique's father stepped up to William. "Well, Monsieur William Hooker, you look just like your father." He embraced William and kissed him on the cheeks. Stepping back, he said, "Welcome to our home, William."

William said, "Thank you, Monsieur Du Mont. I have come for Monique."

Taking William by the arm, Monique's father said, "Well, that's good, but first you must be fatigued from your journey. Let us retire to the kitchen for refreshments."

William followed Monique's father back to the kitchen. There Monique's father showed William to a seat at the kitchen table. Taking a bottle of wine and two glasses, Monique's father had a seat across from him. He then poured a glass of wine for William and himself. Then, looking into William's eyes, he said, "William, we had hoped that letter would have reached you before you begin your journey. Now I must tell you the tragic news. Monique passed away five weeks ago."

William just sat there looking at Monique's father, stunned. The scene took on an aspect of unreality. It was like he was viewing it from outside his body. Like it wasn't really happening. Finally, he said, Monique passed away. How?"

He had to calm his nerves. He reached for the glass of wine, and drank deep. His mind was still reeling. He still couldn't quite bring himself to accept it. How could someone so beautiful and so in love with life be dead.

Monique's father said, "Monique went out to the barn one morning to milk the cows. There was an accident. There was a piece of wood on the floor of the barn, with a nail sticking up from it. Monique stepped on the nail and it went all the way through her foot. Immediately her mother cleaned and dressed the wound as best she could. By that evening Monique had a pounding headache, it was tetanus. I do not want to distress you further by describing the agonies that she had to endure. She breathed her last breath before first light of the sixth day and gave her soul up to God."

William, like most adults, knew about the ravages of tetanus. "You are right, Monsieur Du Mont, I would not like to hear of Monique's agonies."

William now felt his weariness from his travel. He had a need to be alone, to be away from everyone for a while. He needed time alone to come to terms with Monique's passing.

Monique's father, seeing that William needed some time alone, said, "I can see that you are tired from your travel. We have a room for you. Why don't you go up and rest? We will call you for dinner. William just nodded. Monique's mother took William up to his room.

As soon as he was alone in the room. William collapsed on the bed. True he was fatigued from the coach ride from Paris. However, there was no way that he could sleep. All he could think of was Monique dead, lying in the cold ground. All these years corresponding with her, learning to love her from afar. Now, just a few weeks before they would have been together to consummate their marriage, she was taken from him. As he lay alone in the room, he shed tears for the memory of his beloved Monique.

The next day Monique's father took William to visit Monique's grave. The stone had been placed on her grave just days ago. Right away he noticed that the name on the stone was, Monique Du Mont Hooker. He stood at the grave for a few minutes and prayed. Monique's father stood beside him. Knowing Monique as being Catholic, William recited Catholic prayers that he had learned from his mother when he was a child. Monique's father prayed with him. Before he left, William picked up a hand full of dirt and threw it on Monique's grave.

For three days William stayed With Monique's family. He finally unpacked the gifts that his parents and other family members had sent with him for Monique's family. The next morning after breakfast, he presented the gifts to Monique's family. As he presented them, he said, "I know that this isn't the joyous occasion that these gifts were meant for. However, I know that Mom and Dad would still like for you to have them. Being that there is no need for me to stay here anymore. I Will be departing tomorrow for home."

It was after one o-clock in the morning when Madame Gauzet was awakened by someone pounding on the door. The pounding had also awakened Azura. As her mother went to answer the door, Azura got out of bed and grabbed her bundle of clothes that was sitting on the night stand.

Opening the door just a little, Madame Gauzet said, "What is it?"

A woman that worked at the inn stood at the door. Hearing Madame Gauzet, she said, "Madame Gauzet, there are committeemen in the village looking for Azura. There is little time before they will be here."

Madam Gauzet said, "Thank you." Then closed the door.

Azura, only in her nightgown and bare foot, had her bundle of clothes and was coming through her bedroom door. Her mother accompanied her as far as the kitchen. The house was still dark and would remain that way until the committeemen showed up. In the kitchen, Azura's mother grabbed the leftover bread from the evening before, a wedge of brie and some hard sausage from the kitchen counter: wrapped it in a linen cloth and handed it to Azura. She then said, "Run, Azura, get far away as quickly as you can. Remember that I love you."

Azura replied, as she let herself out the kitchen door. "I love you too, Mother."

Once outside, Azura followed the path past the rabbit hutch, privy and tool shed. At the storage shed she paused just long enough to grab her travel bag. She then continued on past the chicken coop and out through the back gate into the woods. She continued on into the woods for over two-hundred meters before she stopped to dress. As she was dressing, she saw the light from lanterns approaching her house from up the road.

After she had dressed, she moved deeper into the woods. She knew these woods well, having gathered dead branches for fire wood and fodder for the rabbits there. There was enough moon light for her to see her way. As soon as she was far enough away from the village, she crossed the road and headed in the direction of Paris.

SIX

The next morning, after breakfast, Monique's father hitched up the gig. As William came out to the gig, all of Monique's family was there to see him off. All of Monique's brothers and sisters said good-bye to him. Monique's mother then handed him a bundle wrapped in a cloth. She said, "William, you had gifts for us. In return I would like to give you this. Most of Monique's clothes were for work here at the inn. These are two special gowns that she had to wear for church or special occasions. Your sister Tandra is Monique's age. They should fit her. We would like for her to have them."

Taking the bundle, William said, "Thank you, Madame Du Mont. I am sure that Tandra will love them."

Monique's mother then gave him a hug and wished him a safe journey. William then boarded the gig and they were off.

When they arrived at the inn, where the coach for Paris would be picking up passengers, William dismounted. Monique's father also dismounted, handed William's bag to him, then shook hands. "Fare-thee-well, William. I wish you a safe and speedy voyage. Tell your father and mother that we are thinking of them."

William responded, "Yes, I shall do that."

Monique's father then embraced William, kissed him on the cheeks, then released him. He then mounted the gig, gave William a wave of the hand and got the horse moving.

A few minutes later, the Paris coach arrived. William found that he would be sharing the inside seats of the coach with an elderly couple and a French Army Captain. They were all going all the way to Paris. After the usual rounds of introduction, William answered a few questions, then saying that he was fatigued, tried to get some rest. This worked only for a couple of hours before he was drawn into the general conversation with the rest of the passengers. It would be near impossible to isolate one's self in such a confined space for almost a day and a half from the other passengers.

William told his story about being married with Monique by proxy. How he had traveled from America to take her back home; and how she had fallen ill and died before he arrived.

Hearing that William was a widower, everyone felt sorry for him. The elderly couple felt it a tragedy that his wife had been taken from him before they could have experienced married life together.

After everyone had said their condolences for his loss; the topic turned to the favorite subject for French men and women, the revolution and politics. William answered questions, but offered no opinions, remembering what his father told him about staying out of local politics. When he was asked a question about America, the American revolution and the American government, he answered them.

Late afternoon the coach arrived in Paris, at the same inn that he had taken the Coach to Reims from. Not wanting to stay at the inn, William made his way to the residence of Monsieur and Madame Minot and was able to rent the carriage house room that he had had before.

After dinner, William went to his room and tried to rest. However, as much as he wanted to, his mind was full of thoughts of Monique. He finally gave up the thought of getting any rest and went for a walk about the neighborhood.

Azura kept going through the night. She kept to the woods when she had to, but was able to cross open fields using the cover of darkness, as long as she was far enough away from houses where there might be dogs to give an alarm.

Towards the first light of morning, Azura found a place in the woods where she wasn't likely to be disturbed and got a few hours' sleep. She slept lightly, coming awake at every sound. It wasn't very restful, but it was at least some help.

Towards the afternoon, after a quick meal of the bread, brie and sausage, she got on the move again. She made use of the woods afforded whenever she could. When she had to cross an open space, she would cross as far away from where people might be to observe or question her.

After sun down she kept on going, staying in or close to the woods when-ever possible. By first light she could see the outskirts of Paris. She stopped to get some rest in a secluded spot in the woods. She would rest, then enter the city in late afternoon. That way she could blend in with people going home from work or shopping.

In mid-afternoon, Azura got up and brushed herself and her clothing off as best she could to make herself presentable. She then took her travel bag and started out. Within the hour she was among the houses at the edge of the city. Azura had spent most of her time in Versailles, or Madame Du Barry's private estates. She knew very little about Paris, or anyone that lived there. She would just have to make her way the best she could, but first she would need a place to stay.

Azura had first wanted to get further into the city. She needed to be where she could find a place to stay. She also needed to be around where people congregated. She had to find out how she could obtain travel documents. She had no idea as to how she would do that. She would just have to keep her eyes and ears open and trust to luck.

It was after dark before she came in sight of an inn. Although this area was mostly residential with some shops, she hadn't seen any room for rent signs. Perhaps she could spend the night at the inn. She hoped that they didn't check the papers of those seeking lodging at the inn. She would just have to risk it.

She was about to pass an alleyway, when two men sprang out in front of her. One was of slight build, with dark hair and beard, a slender rat-like face and cunning eyes. The second was an enormous bear of a man, a full head taller than his partner, with dark hair and beard. The smaller man said, "Well, Mademoiselle, where might you be going at this time of night?"

Azura tried to go around them, but the larger man grabbed her arm in a vice-like grip. He then said, "Well, Raous, what do we have here?"

The smaller man responded. "What do you think, Delman, could she be wanted by the Committee?"

Azura's blood turned cold at the mention of the Committee.

The larger man laughed, then said, "Perhaps we take her in. There might be a reward for her."

Now Azura was really frightened and the men could see it.

The smaller man said, "Perhaps, then perhaps not. If she can give us an enjoyable time, we might just let her go."

They started to drag her back into the alleyway. They were groping her through her clothing. One man had his hand on her breast. The other had his hand on her vulva. She started to scream.

William was walking down the street, headed back to his room in the carriage house, when he heard a woman scream. It was coming from an alleyway just up ahead. Without any thought as to rather he should involve himself in local matters, he rushed toward the woman's screams. Entering the alleyway, he saw two men assaulting a young woman. Without a pause, he raised his walking stick and charged.

The smaller man, hearing someone approach, turned to see who it was. William swung the butt of his cane, aiming generally at the man's head. You could call it a lucky shot; the plumb size brass knob on the butt of the cane caught the man in the throat, crushing his larynx. The man started to sink to the cobble stones holding his throat, as he tried to breathe.

The larger man, sensing danger, turned to face William and pulled a large knife with about a six or seven-inch blade. William, seeing the knife, swung his walking stick with all the force that he could put behind it. The walking stick struck the man on the wrist, causing him to drop the knife. Without his knife, the large man rushed William, catching him in a bearhug. He soon had William on the cobble stones fighting for his life.

Azura, now being ignored, due to William's intervention, watched the large man trying to crush William with his brute strength. Seeing the knife that the larger man had dropped on the pavement. Azura took the knife in both hands and raising it over her head, drove the blade into the man's back. The blade slipped between two ribs and sliced through the heart. The man immediately went into shock and lost consciousness.

William rolled the man off him and with effort, stood up. He could see that the young woman was trembling from the shock of the experience. He knew how the woman must feel, he had also never killed a man before. He knew that he had to take charge and get her mind on something else, before she collapsed into a fit of sobbing. He said, "Are you all right?"

Azura looked at him, with a wide-eyed stare. He shook her shoulders. Finally, she focused on him. "Yes, I'm all right. They restrained and groped me, but you came along in time to prevent them from raping me. I wish to thank you, Monsieur."

Pointing to the two dead bodies, William said, "We must hide the bodies."

Looking around, he saw some empty crates and other refuse further back in the alleyway. Pointing to the larger man, he said, "You grab one foot and I'll grab the other. We will then drag him back behind those crates."

After they had dragged the two dead men behind the empty crates, they covered the bodies with some trash to hide them. William then turned to Azura, "Mademoiselle, do you live close by here?"

Azura shook her head. "No, Monsieur, I do not live in Paris. I can't go home."

Presenting his arm to her, he said, "Then come with me."

She took his arm and he led her out of the alleyway, picking up her travel bag on the way. It was but a short three blocks to William's room in the carriage house. Going through the garden gate, William unlocked the door to the room and led Azura inside. He turned up the lamp on the small table in the room and had Azura take a seat in a chair at the table. Taking a bottle of wine and two glasses, William sat across from her. He filled both glasses with wine. He then pushed one glass towards her. "Here, drink this." He said.

Azura took the glass offered and took a swallow of wine. It felt warm going down; and had a calming effect on her.

After taking a drink of wine himself, William said, "We have things to discuss, but first I believe introductions are in order. I am William Hooker; and you are?"

Azura for the first time took a good look at William. She saw a young man perhaps three to four years older than she was. He had black hair and dark-blue eyes. He was handsome and well dressed. She said, "My name is Azura Gauzet."

William saw a young woman of fair complexion, ice-blue eyes, pail-blonde hair down past her shoulder blades and with a very attractive face. Looking at her across the table, he said, "First off, you said that you didn't live in Paris and that you couldn't go home. Why is that?"

Azura looked at him. She had determined that although he spoke the language fluently, he wasn't French. Perhaps he was English. She decided to take a risk on him. Looking back at him, she said, "Two days ago committeemen came to my village to arrest me. My mother and I were warned and I fled. I came to Paris to try and get travel documents, so that I can go to England."

William wanted to know more, he said, "Well, Mademoiselle Gauzet, why would the Committee for Public Safety want to arrest you?"

Azura said, "I was in the service of Madame Marie Jeanne Du Barry. Someone must have denounced me as a royalist sympathizer."

"And once you got to Paris, how did you plan to get travel Documents?" William said.

Azura shrugged her shoulders. "I don't know. I guess just look around for someone looking to sale travel documents."

William got up and started to pace the floor. His father had warned him, to not get involved in local affairs. Now, because he had come to this woman's rescue, they were both responsible in the death of two men. The bodies were hidden for now, but they would soon start to smell. If he turned this woman out, she would most likely be in custody within twenty-four hours. Like it or not, their destinies had become intertwined. To ensure his own safety, he would have to help her to escape the Committee of Public Safety. After a few minutes, he decided on what to do.

He took the documents from his bag and sat back down at the table. Looking at Azura, he said. "Mademoiselle Gauzet, I am an American, I live in Newport, Rhode Island. I came to France to get my bride and take her back to America with me. Unfortunately, she died about five weeks before I arrived." Pointing to the documents on the table, he continued, "These are passports and travel documents for myself and my wife Monique. With these I can get you safely out of France and to America. All you have to do is pretend to be my bride. Will you do it?"

Azura thought for a while. She had planned to go to England. That was where her mother had told her to go. However, America was a place where she would be safe and free to build a new life. Finally, she said, "Thank you, Monsieur Hooker, I will do it."

William reached out and patted her hand. "Good, now you understand that traveling as husband and wife, we must be convincing as husband and wife. That means that we must show affection for each other; and when we take a room for the night at an inn, we must share the same bed."

Azura exclaimed, "Share the same bed, Monsieur! I am a virgin! I have never known a man! That is out of the question!"

William responded, "It is necessary, any maid can tell how many people slept in a bed. Now, if you are concerned about your virtue, this I shall promise you on my personal honor. I shall always respect your virtue and not use my position as your protector to have my way with you. I will defend your person and virtue against any threat. I will never abandon you in favor of my own wellbeing. As long as you are with me, no harm shall come to you."

Azura thought for a while. He was asking a lot of her, to have faith in him, to trust his word of honor. However, he had come to her rescue, at his own peril; and if she turned him down, would she ever be able to get papers to leave France. Finally, if he were to take advantage of her, was her virtue worth more than her liberty, even perhaps her life? At last, she nodded to William. "Yes, Monsieur, I can see the wisdom and necessity of it. I shall do as you say."

Later, as they got ready for bed, Azura still wasn't comfortable being in bed with a man. She insisted that they sleep in their clothing; and also sleep with a sheet between them, she over and he under the sheet. Later in bed Azura felt nervous being in bed with a man. However, after a few minutes when nothing happened, she started to relax and was soon asleep.

SEVEN

Williiam and Azura awoke early the next morning, just as the first-faint light started to come in through the windows. Azura had slept in her clothing, removing only her shoes. William had removed his cutaway coat, waistcoat, cravat and shoes.

As he put on his shoes, he took a look at Azura, her gown was that of the fashion worn by the working class, made of an indigo dyed linen. It was also soiled by two days on the road and sleeping in the woods, he said, "Azura, do you have anything any better in your travel bag to wear?"

Azura responded, "I have one other gown, much the same as this one, but cleaner."

William then thought of the bundle that he had been given by Monique's mother. Removing it from his travel bag, he opened it. Inside were two gowns. One was of a fine linen floral print with an apricot background. The other was of a lapis-blue silk-brocade. Showing the two gowns to Azura, he said. These two gowns belonged to my wife, if they fit you, you can wear them. Now I shall go in to the main house to get some hot water for us to clean up and for me to shave. You can get dressed while I am gone."

William went to the kitchen of the main house to get hot water from Madame Minot. She asked if he wanted to have breakfast with them. William thanked her, then said that he would eat at the inn before he took the coach. She ended up wrapping some bread and cheese in a couple of sheets of newspaper for him. William thanked her and returned to the carriage house room.

When William got back to the room, Azura had changed into the floral print gown. There had also been an apricot color bonnet to match the gown in the bundle; and also, a lapis-blue bonnet to match the other gown. To this she had added a white-lace fichu. He was struck by how so much more attractive she looked with a night's rest and a new gown.

William had brought from the kitchen of the main house a large pitcher of hot water, wash rag and small towel. He poured a small amount of water in his shaving mug. The rest he poured into a basin on the night table by the wall, where a small mirror hung. He then took his shaving brush and started to work up a lather in his shaving mug. He then lathered up his face and started to scrape the lather and short growth of beard with his razor.

Azura watched him shave with rap fascination. Growing up in a house of only women, she had never seen a man shave before. She wondered how it felt to have the sharp edge of a razor so close to your skin. When he had finished, she couldn't resist touching his cheek to see how smooth the skin was. After they both used the water in the basin to freshen up their face, neck and hands, William through the water out.

William then put on his cravat, waistcoat and cutaway coat. He then turned to Azura and said, "Now Azura, from this moment on you are no longer Mademoiselle Azura Gauzet. You are now Madame Monique Du Mont Hooker, my wife. Please do not forget it. I shall address you as Monique, my wife, or any other name of affection. You may call me William, my husband, or any other name of affection. In public we must act with familiarity as husband and wife. Can you do that?"

Azura nodded. "Yes, My Husband, I can do that."

Up to now they had been conversing only in French. William said, "By the way, do you speak English?"

Azura replied, "Yes, My Husband, I speak English; I also speak Italian and Spanish. My mistress Madame Du Barry used me to eavesdrop on guest to get information. To the guests I was just another servant, with no ear for languages."

William laughed, then said, "You must have been valuable to your mistress."

Azura nodded, "Well, she took good care of me."

William put on his top hat, took his walking stick and travel bag. "Well, My Wife, let us be off."

Azura took her travel bag and followed William out of the room and through the garden gate to the street. There William offered her his arm; and they walked arm and arm to the inn.

At the inn they reserved seats on the coach to Orleans. They then had breakfast of Raspberry preserves, bread brie and coffee with milk and beet sugar. The coffee was drinkable, although William would rather like to have some cane sugar for his coffee.

After breakfast they went out to the front court-yard to wait on the coach. Standing there waiting, William put his arm about her waist and pulled her into his shoulder. She placed her hand on his wrist and lay her head on his shoulder. William was pleased that she was playing the part of the loving spouse.

A few minutes later the coach for Orleans arrived. William put the travel bags in the coach, then helped Azura to board. Two other men boarded the coach. One was a young army captain, not much older than William. The other was an older man. They were both going on this coach as far as Orleans. After introductions, William found out that the elder man lived in Orleans. The young captain was going on to Montlucon to join his regiment. They became really interested in William as soon as they found out that he was an American.

As soon as the coach was loaded, they were off. They were soon on the main road from Paris to Orleans. Since they were south of the heart of the city, they were traveling through mostly small business and residential districts. At this hour of the morning, there were many people on the streets going to work, or shopping.

As they reached the outskirts of the city, they encountered a barricade (A road block where every-one traveling the road had to stop to have their travel documents checked). At the sight of the barricade, Azura grabbed William's hand. William could feel her anxiety from how hard she was squeezing his hand. He whispered a word of encouragement in her ear, then kissed her lightly on the lips. She smiled at him and her grip loosened on his hand.

The Barricade was manned by three committeemen, most likely Jacobins, wearing their 'Bonnet Rouge' or red cap of liberty, with a pistol or knife stuck in their belts. There were also two National Guard Soldiers in uniform with musket and bayonet.

When one of the committeemen opened the door of the coach to check everyone's travel documents, William handed him the travel documents for himself and Monique, saying, "I am an American. I and my wife are traveling to Nantes to take ship to America."

The committeeman gave their papers a cursory look, seeing the stamps and seals. He then returned the papers to William, saying, "Welcome to France citizen; have a pleasant journey."

As he put the papers back into an inside coat pocket, William nodded. "Thank you, citizen."

The committeeman then checked the travel documents of the other inside passengers and found them in order. Once the travel documents of the other passengers that were riding on the outside of the coach were checked, the coach was waved on its way.

As the coach continued on, William pulled Azura towards him, she relaxed, putting her head on his shoulder. She now felt confident that their travel documents would hold up to inspection by the committeemen manning the barricades. She knew that most of the committeemen on the barricades were barely literate; what they looked for in the documents was the stamps and seals. They looked first at the persons hands, then at their papers. If the person said that they were a carpenter, kitchen worker, field worker, or maid they should have rough-calloused hands. If they had soft hands without callouses, they were taken off the coach for interrogations.

Once everyone in the coach became acquainted, they begin to talk to pass the time. Once it was learned that William was an American traveling back to America with his wife, Monique, the two other passengers wanted to know all about America. In the conversations Azura played the role of the shy new bride, deferring to her husband on most questions.

William was asked how the United States of America had managed to have a stable government so quickly after their War for Independence. William told them that the former colonies already had a legacy of self-government before they broke away from Britain. France was having to learn that it was far easier to overthrow a tyrant than to govern themselves. William also explained how they had first tried to govern by articles of confederation. When that didn't work, they called a convention and created the Constitution of the United States. The constitution lay the foundation for a stable government.

The people then elected General George Washington as their President and Head of State.

The Captain, being a military man, then asked William about the American Army. William told him that after the war with Britain, the United States mustered out all the regiments of the continental line. The Federal Army is now less than one-hundred men, that are used mostly to guard military equipment, weapons and ammunition depots. When the captain asked about the defense of the nation, William told him that the United States relied on the State Militia for national defense. The French Captain found it a most unusual way to conduct a defense.

The coach rolled on all that day, through the night and most of the following day. The coach stopped only to give the passengers some time to move around and have a meal, to change horses or drivers. During the night William sat back into the corner of the seat. Azura lay against him, drew her feet up on the seat and slept with her head on his shoulder.

It was late afternoon when the coach arrived at an inn in Orleans. William had decided that they would get a room at the inn and rest, before continuing on in the morning. Finding the inn keeper in the common room, William said, "Monsieur Inn Keeper, my wife and I would like to have a room for the night."

The inn keeper responded, "Yes, Monsieur, we have rooms available." He then quoted the price for the room.

William paid for the room and received the key, then said. "We will be traveling on to Tours, then on to Nantes. When does the coach for Tours leave in the morning?"

The inn keeper responded, "The coach for Tours leaves at ten in the morning."

William said, "Thank you, Monsieur Inn Keeper."

William and Azura first dropped off their travel bags in their room; then went to the common room for dinner. The inn was serving lamb stew, with green salad, bread and wine. As fatigued as they were, they didn't much notice how good the meal was. They just wanted to satisfy their hunger, before getting some rest.

After dinner, they went back to their room. William let Azura go in and get undressed and ready for bed first. A few minutes later he entered the room. Azura was already in bed. He noticed that she had undressed and was wearing a night gown. At least she was willing to go along with the plan to pretend to be his wife. She had her back to him so that he could have some privacy while getting ready for bed. After turning the lamp down for the night, he quickly got undressed and into his night shirt. Getting into bed, he made sure to sleep with his back to her as she was sleeping with her back to him.

Neither William or Azura were able to get to sleep right away. They each had to overcome the feelings that they had sleeping next to each other. William felt her presence, however, having lost Monique only recently, he had little desire for another woman. However, having Azura next to him in the coach for hour after hour. To have her lean into him. To feel her body press against his. He couldn't help but to take an interest in her. He was finding out that not only was she attractive; she was also very intelligent and had an aptitude for language, a very valuable asset. He still mourned for Monique. However, it seemed that now, when he tried to think of Monique, the image of Azura came to mind. Why was he having trouble picturing Monique in his mind. He didn't want to disrespect Monique's memory. He would just have to keep telling himself that his and Azura's familiarity was just an act.

Azura, having never known a man before, in the biblical sense, felt uneasy in bed with a man. It was even harder, now that she was starting to know William, and had found him to be a very likeable person. He was a handsome man, that was self-assured and brave. He also had wit and charm. He was a man that she could fall in love with. That made it even harder to resist him, but she would have to.

After a while exhaustion took over and they slept.

EIGHT

Azura awoke first the next morning. Getting out of bed, she quickly dressed. After checking in the mirror that hung on the wall behind the night stand that her hair was properly arranged, she left the room.

Going to the kitchen, Azura encountered the inn keeper's wife, who was supervising the kitchen staff as they got ready for another day's work. Azura said, "Madame, might I have some hot water, so that my husband can shave?"

Looking at Azura, the inn keeper's wife responded, "Why of course, Madame, I shall get you some hot water right away."

The inn keeper's wife took a pitcher and filled it with hot water from a cauldron of boiling water. She then handed the pitcher, along with a wash cloth and small towel to Azura. "Here is your hot water, Madame, with our complements."

Taking the pitcher of hot water, wash cloth and towel from the inn keeper's wife, Azura said, "Merci, Madame."

Azura hurried back to the room with the hot water. Arriving there, she found that William was up and already dressed in shirt, breeches, hose and shoes. Azura placed the pitcher on the night stand, next to a porcelain basin.

William took the pitcher and poured most of the hot water into the porcelain basin. He then poured just enough into his shaving mug to work up a lather. He then lathered up his face and begin to shave. Azura watched him shave with acute attention, as she used the hot water and wash cloth to wash her face, neck and hands.

As she watched him shave, Azura considered the relationship that was developing between William and herself. At first the play acting of treating him as her spouse and addressing him as 'My Husband' felt strange to her. Now, when she says 'My Husband', it seemed so natural to her. He had offered his help to her, without any request for anything in return for it. He had even refused her offer to share the expenses. So far, he had been an honorable man, respecting her person. He had become her champion, her shield against all that would seek to do her harm. He had earned her respect and more. She found herself admiring him. She wondered how it would be to really be his wife; to really share the bed pleasures with him. She was falling in love with him. However, there was a barrier between them. The ghost of his deceased wife seemed to be foremost on his mind. How could you compete against a spirit?

After William finished shaving, he washed his face, neck and hands. He then finished dressing, putting on his cravat, waistcoat and cutaway coat. He then put on his top hat and took his walking cane. Azura put on her fichu and bonnet.

William then said, "Well, My Wife, let us go and have breakfast."

Azura nodded. "Yes, My Husband, let us do that."

In the common room breakfast was already laid out for the inn's guests. There was coffee. with milk and beet sugar in pitchers, bread, butter, strawberry preserves and brie. After filling their cups with coffee and fixing their plates; they took seats at a table to eat their breakfast. William had chosen a table off in a corner that was far enough away from the other guest to have some privacy. As they ate, they talked.

William said, "Tell me a little about yourself, like your family."

Azura swallowed the bread and brie that she had been chewing on. "Well, My Husband, to start out, my mother has four children, all girls. I am the youngest. I was born four years after my mother's husband died. My mother said that my father was a young soldier, that just happened to be around when she felt the need for someone. By the time she found that she was pregnant and needed to remember his name, she had forgotten it. My mother said that my blue eyes and pale-blonde hair is my legacy from my father. My mother lives in a small village not far from Versailles. Now, My Husband, what about your family?"

William put down his coffee cup. "Well, My Wife, my family lives in Newport, Rhode Island. My father owns a general store there. He also owns farms and other property in and around Newport. He is also part owner in some ships. I have an older brother, Thomas, who will inherit the store. My father has given me a farm of fifty-seven acres, that's about twenty-three hectares, with a house and barn. My mother is French-Canadian from Quebec Provence. I have other brothers and sisters. They are in order of birth, Tandra, Samuel, Clark, Jelline and Ninon."

Azura said, "With a farm like that you are a rich man."

William nodded. "Yes, it is a good farm, but I am not a farmer."

"Not a farmer," Azura said, "then what do you do?"

William took another sip of coffee, then said, "I am an avocat. I am an associate to an older and more experienced avocat in Newport."

William didn't have to ask her about what work she did. He had learned all about her being in the service of Madame Du Barry that first night, after he had rescued her from her assailants. They spent the rest of the time in the common room, talking more about their families. After hearing about his mother from William, Azura felt sure that she would really like his mother

After breakfast, they got their bags from their room, then went out to the front court of the inn to wait for the coach. They stood side by side, with an arm about each other's waist. This closeness had started out as being play acting, but by now had started to seem natural to them. By now, even though they hadn't admitted it to each other, they each now yearned for the nearness of the other. Anyone observing them would believe that they were not other that what they appeared to be; a young, loving, married couple.

The coach arrived on time; and they boarded it. There were two other passengers that boarded with them. Right away William became suspicious of them. The couple were both in their mid-thirties, as best he could judge their ages. They were dressed as common members of the working class. However, they didn't look as if they have spent a lifetime in hard drudgery. They were not very talkative, preferring to keep to themselves.

At the first stop, just after the noon hour, they had the time to take care of their needs; and get a quick meal. William and Azura had the opportunity to speak in private. William said, "Well, My Wife, what do you think of our fellow passengers?"

Azura responded, "Well, My Husband, I do not think that they are as what they are trying to pass themselves off as."

That was William's thought also. "Then, My Wife, do you think that they are members of the nobility?"

Azura thought for a moment. "Perhaps, My Husband, the man could have a minor title, or most likely, they are servants of some rank. Whatever they are, they are most likely being sought by the Committee of Public Safety. I would say that it is best that we have nothing to do with them."

William nodded. "Yes, My Wife, I agree with you. It should not be too hard, being that they already want to keep to themselves. Now, if anything happens, just keep calm and do as I do, or as I tell you to do."

Taking his arm, she said, "Yes, My Husband, I shall do as you say."

The two bodies lay exposed on the cobble stones of the alleyway. All the gendarmeries that were close to the bodies were holding handkerchiefs to their faces. Monsieur Proust, an agent of the Committee of Public Safety, was speaking with the senior gendarmerie on the scene. "Tell me Inspector, how did they find the bodies?"

The senior gendarmerie said, "People started to notice an objectionable odor coming from the alleyway. Looking, they found the bodies buried under some rubbish, behind some empty crates. That's when we found out about them."

Putting a scented handkerchief up to his face, Monsieur Proust moved closer to get a better look. He then moved back to the senior gendarmerie. "I know these men, Inspector. They were the dregs of society, but they had a knack for sniffing out people wanted by the committee. They would bring people to us. If they were wanted, we would give them enough of a reward for them to buy some wine and get drunk. If some of the women were a little disheveled, well, I'm not going to chastise them for rough handling of a wanted fugitive."

"Then, Monsieur Proust, you know who they are?" The senior gendarmerie said.

Looking at the two bodies, Monsieur Proust said, "I do know them by their first names. The big fellow's name is Delman. His small-rat faced friend is Raous. Their last names were not important to me, being that they were not social equals. However, they were citizens; so, we must find out who was responsible for this crime."

The senior gendarmerie said, "Monsieur Proust, I have had men knocking on doors, trying to find out if anyone saw or heard anything two or three days ago, I estimate that they have been dead for at least that long. However, I don't have much hope of finding out anything that way. Most people keep their shutters closed when they hear a commotion outside."

Just then the doctor acting as coroner arrived. After a quick inspection of the bodies; he went to speak with the senior gendarmerie and Monsieur Proust.

"Well, Doctor," Monsieur Proust said, "what do you have to say as to the manner of death."

Glancing back at the two bodies, the doctor replied, "It is for certain by the knife in his back is how the big man died. I would say that the knife went between the ribs and through the heart. Although I would have to confirm that at autopsy. The person that used that knife had to be very good with it, or very lucky. Now the little guy, I didn't see any marks on him. I shall have to do a more thorough examination of the body to determine the cause of death."

As Monsieur Proust was speaking to the doctor, another gendarmerie entered the alleyway and spoke with the senior gendarmerie. The senior gendarmerie called to Monsieur Proust, "Monsieur Proust, this man has something important to say."

Monsieur Proust looked at the gendarmerie. "Well, what is it!"

The gendarmerie resisted taking a step back, in reaction to Monsieur Proust's abrupt manner. "Well, Monsieur Proust. I just questioned a woman across the street. She told me that she heard a woman scream three nights ago. At first, she was afraid to look. Finally, after a few minutes, she looked out her window. She observed a man and woman on the street, walking toward the inn. The man was carrying a travel bag."

The gendarmerie had gotten Monsieur Proust attention. "Was she able to give you an identification? Their appearance, age, build, hair color?"

The gendarmerie shook his head. "No, Monsieur Proust. She said that it was too dark to see anything more than the forms of a man and woman walking down the street. She did add after some questioning that they seemed to be a young couple."

Monsieur Proust turned to the doctor. "Doctor, if you please, let me know as soon as you have a cause of death for the other man."

The doctor nodded. "Yes, Monsieur Proust."

To the senior gendarmerie. He said, "Let us go to the inn and see if they know anything about this couple."

Monsieur Proust and the senior gendarmerie quickly walked the three blocks to the inn. When they got there, they sought out the inn keeper. Monsieur Proust introduced himself. "Monsieur Inn Keeper. I am Monsieur Proust, an agent of the Committee of Public Safety."

The inn keeper, seeing the gendarmerie and hearing the words, Agent of the Committee of Public Safety, begin to perspire nervously. "Yes, Monsieur Proust, how may I assist you."

Monsieur Proust said, "Monsieur Inn Keeper, I'm looking for a young couple that might have stayed here, or taken the coach from here about three days ago."

The inn keeper thought for over a minute, before he answered, "I don't know, Monsieur Proust. People come through here all the time, it is hard to remember who was through here only yesterday. One thing though that I can tell you, there were no young coupled guesting at the inn three nights ago."

Monsieur Proust was about to say something, when the inn keeper continued, "Now I do remember a young couple, newly-weds, that took the coach to Orleans three days ago."

The inn keeper now had Monsieur Proust's interest. Monsieur Proust said, "Monsieur Inn Keeper, do you remember what they looked like?"

The inn keeper thought for a few seconds, then shook his head. "No, Monsieur Proust, I do not recall them. They didn't guest at the inn. They just showed up that morning, had breakfast, then took the coach to Orleans."

Monsieur Proust knew what he had to do; he would have to pursue them. "Monsieur Inn Keeper, when is the next coach to Orleans?"

The inn keeper replied, "That would be at ten in the morning, Monsieur Proust."

Monsieur Proust said, "Monsieur Inn Keeper, I want a seat on the coach for Orleans in the morning."

After arranging for a seat on the coach to Orleans in the morning; Monsieur Proust went to see the doctor that was acting as coroner for the double murder. By the time he arrived, the doctor had been able to determine the cause of death for both of the victims.

After the greetings, the doctor said, "Monsieur Proust, I know the cause of death for both of the victims."

Monsieur Proust was pleased by the competence and efficiency of the doctor. He wished that everyone that he had dealings with was so. "Well, Doctor, what was the cause of death?"

The doctor said, "Well, first, the man that was stabbed, he was stabbed with his own knife. I found the sheath for the knife under his coat. The other man had a crushed larynx. He died by asphyxiation. He couldn't get air in or out of his lungs."

Monsieur Proust looked the doctor in the eyes. "Doctor, could they have been killed by a young couple, a man and woman?"

The doctor thought for few seconds, then nodded. "Yes, Monsieur Proust, it could have happened that way. The smaller man had no other marks on him. He could have been taken by surprise, and his larynx crushed before he could respond. With him out of the way, it would be two on one."

Monsieur Proust was now sure that he had to run down that young couple that left for Orleans. He took his leave from the doctor; and went home to pack a travel bag.

The coach was about fifteen kilometers from Blois, when they encountered a barricade. It was manned by three committeemen and two National Guard Soldiers with muskets and bayonets. As soon as the coach came to a stop, the door on the other side of the coach from where William was sitting was opened by a committeeman.

The committeeman said. "Your papers, citizen!"

The other man in the coach presented the papers for him and his wife to the committeeman. The committeeman took the papers and took a quick look at them. He then asked. "What is your occupation, Monsieur; and why are you and your wife traveling to Nantes?"

William could see that the man and his wife were becoming tense. He took Azura's hand in his and gave her a reassuring glance.

The other man said, "Well, Monsieur, I am a warehouse worker. My wife and I are returning to Nantes after a visit with family in Orleans."

The committeeman grabbed one of the man's hands and turned it palm up. "I think not, monsieur. Being a warehouse worker is hard work. All these hands have ever lifted is a wine glass and ladies petticoats."

With a jerk, the committeeman pulled the man from the coach. Another man grabbed the man's wife to remove her from the coach. The woman screamed as she was dragged from the coach.

William could feel Azura tense in fear. He gave her a reassuring smile and squeeze of the hand.

The committeeman then held his hand out to William. "Your Papers, Monsieur!"

William handed over the travel documents and passports for himself and Monique. The man took a quick look at the papers, then said, "You are Americans, Monsieur?"

William said, "Yes, my wife and I are on our way to Nantes to take ship back to America."

With a smile, the committeeman handed the papers back to William. "Welcome to France, citizen."

William gave him a cordial nod. "Thank you, citizen."

As the coach pulled away from the barricade, Azura started to relax.

NINE

The coach made a stop at an inn in Blois to change horses. It already was late afternoon; and William wasn't looking forward to another overnight coach ride. He decided to take a room at the inn here in Blois for the night. Afterall, they were not far from Nantes, and he was no longer so concerned about pursuit. Azura by now had come to trust William's judgement and readily agreed.

After getting a room at the inn. They took the time to go for a stroll about and see what some of the shops in town had to offer, before having dinner. They soon came to a lady's hatter and appraised the wares displayed in the window. There was a marvelous display in the shop window of lady's hats. William decided to enter and see whatever else there was to offer.

Madame Girard heard the bell over the door jingle and looked to see a young man and woman enter her shop. The way that they were arm in arm, she took them for a married couple. "Good afternoon, Monsieur, Madame, I am Madame Girard. How may I help you?"

William said, "I am Monsieur William Hooker," Indicating Azura, he continued, "and this is my wife, Monique. We looked at what you had in the window, and came in to see what else you have to offer."

Madame Girard could see that, by their dress and bearing, this young couple could possibly have the money to spend on something more than what was necessary. With a smile, Madame Girard said, "Well, Monsieur, Madame, I have a large selection of high-quality hats. I would be glad to serve you."

"Thank you, Madame," William said, "We shall just have a look around."

William and Azura slowly moved about the shop, with Madame Girard close at hand. Most of what Madame Girard had to offer were the bonnets and other hats that were seen most on the street. The quality was good. However, they were what everyone else was wearing. William was about to go, when he spotted a hat that really caught his eye. It was a silver-gray felt hat with a suitably high crown, wide-flat brim, turned down slightly in front. It had a wide-satin teal-blue ribbon as a hat band with a bow in the back, with the tails of the bow hanging down the back. What really caught his eye was that it was also decorated with the tips of peacock feathers that showed the eye in the feathers,

Pointing at the hat, William said, "Madame, may my wife try on that hat?"

Madame Girard reached for the hat. It was the most expensive hat that she had in the shop. She had acquired this hat in expectation of selling it at a good profit. She had been sure that there would be more that one woman in Blois that would want it. As it turned out, People were put off by the price. The hat had turned out to be her white elephant. Now all she hoped to do was to get her money back. Presenting the hat to William, she said, "Yes, Monsieur, Madame may try on the hat." As William took the hat, she pointed and continued, "There is a mirror over there, so that Madame can see how the hat looks on her."

William handed the hat to Azura to try on. Azura put the hat on, and stood before the mirror. Seeing her reflection in the mirror, her face lit up with delight. It was a beautiful hat, equal to the hats worn by the ladies in Versailles. She would love to have it, but she had no right to ask William to purchase it for her. As she turned away from the mirror, she tried not to show how much she desired the hat. However, William had already seen her reaction when she had looked at herself in the mirror; and could tell that she really wanted it.

Turning to the shop keeper, he said, "Madame, what are you asking for this hat?'

Madame Girard quoted a price that would give her a good profit, hoping that she could get a price close to it.

William came back with a counter offer that he knew was lower that the Madame wanted for the hat. The dickering went on back and forth for several minutes. William knew that the price was based on the paper money that was in use now. Not silver or gold coin, that was not subject to the inflated value of the paper money.

Finally, William slapped a good old Yankees silver dollar down on the counter. "Will this be enough for the hat, Madame?"

Madame Girard looked at the silver dollar, and tried not to smile. Unlike the almost worthless paper money that was being used now. Silver and gold coin would keep its value. Taking the coin, she said, "Yes, monsieur, this will be enough."

Azura didn't have to pretend to show her pleasure. She embraced William and kissed him ardently. "Thank you, My Husband. I love my new hat."

William beamed with pleasure at Azura's reaction. He had not entered the shop with the intension of getting anything. However, when he saw Azura with that hat on, he had known that he just had to get it for her. He had started out doing something to help her, by offering to take her to America with him. It now seemed that in helping her, she was doing something for him in turn. Life no longer seemed so hopeless. He still grieved for Monique. However, he no longer felt that his life was over. He now knew that he could live and love again. "It is always my pleasure to please you, My Wife."

Before they left the shop, Madame Girard gave Azura a hat box for her hat. Azura wanted to wear her new hat, putting her old bonnet in the hat box.

Outside the shop, Azura said, "I thank you for the hat, My Husband, I just love it. It is the most wonderful gift that anyone has ever given me; but why did you buy it for me?"

William thought for a moment. He had bought the hat to please her; but was that the only reason? Was it that he was starting to have feelings for her? Finally, he said, "Well, for one thing, it looks just marvelous on you. I just couldn't imagine any other woman wearing that hat. Last of all, I just wanted to please you."

Azura wanted to speak, but she choked up with emotion. Finally, she put her arms about his neck, pulled his face down to hers and kissed him on the lips with passion.

When the kiss was ended, William said, "Wow, I should buy you gifts more often."

Azura smiled. "I just wanted to show my gratitude for the gift."

Arm in arm they turned back to the inn.

For dinner, the inn had fresh-baked carp, with salad, vegetables, bread and wine. Azura wore her new hat to dinner. She wanted to show off William's gift to her. William couldn't help but to admire her. He still didn't know why he did it. He was still in mourning for Monique, but he wasn't dead. He could still recognize a pretty woman. When he saw her face when she tried the hat on, he knew that she had to have it. It also lifted his own spirits by pleasing her.

Azura also studied William as they had dinner. At first, she had thought that his mourning over a lost wife, that he had never met, had dulled his interest in other women. However, she now knew that it wasn't that, he really was a man of honor and would never take advantage of her. She couldn't help it; even though their relationship was just platonic, to convince those that they come in contact with that they are a married couple, she had started to be drawn to him. She couldn't help herself; the more that she got to know him, the more she came to admire him. He was not just an honorable man, but also generous and caring. She had started to wonder just how it would be to really be his wife. In their public play acting, she was starting to become confused as to what was play acting and what was their true feelings toward each other.

After dinner, they walked about the gardens of the inn for a while, then went to their room to get ready for bed. William let Azura get ready for bed first, while he found reasons to be out of the room.

When he returned to the room, Azura was in bed and the lamp was turned down really low. As William disrobed to get ready for bed, Azura took a peek at him in the buff before he put on his night shirt. She had never seen a man in a state of undress before. The sight of William excited her; and at the same time made her ashamed that she had taken such liberties without his knowledge. As he slid into the bed, it was hard for her to ignore his presence beside her and turn her back to him.

William had also become aware of Azura as a woman. However, he still mourned for Monique, was he disrespecting her memory by having thoughts about Azura. Also, he had given his word as a gentleman to Azura that he would not take advantage of her. He had to honor his word to her.

They each battled with their thoughts for the other for awhile, until they drifted off to sleep.

The next morning Azura was the first to arise. She quickly dressed, then went to the inn's kitchen. There she found the inn keeper's wife supervising the kitchen staff. Stepping up to the inn keeper's wife, Azura said, "Madame, may I have some hot water so that my husband can shave?"

The inn keeper's wife gave her a nod. "Of course, Madame, I shall get it for you right away."

"Merci, Madame." Azura said.

A few minutes later, Azura returned to the room with a pitcher of hot water, a wash cloth and a small towel. William was out of bed and dressed in shirt. Breeches, hose and shoes. Azura poured some hot water into the basin on the night stand, then took the wash rag to wash clean her face, neck and hands. William got his shaving kit and started to work up a lather in his shaving mug.

Azura watched him as he shaved, still enthralled by it all. She found this masculine ritual of shaving most intriguing. She wondered if shaving was uncomfortable for the skin. She had no idea what it would feel like to scrape her skin with the sharp edge of a razor. After shaving William finished dressing.

When they both were ready, they left the room. In the common room of the inn, breakfast was already laid out on the tables. It was the usual fair of hot coffee in pitchers with milk and beet sugar, bread brie, butter and this morning apricot preserves.

After they had breakfast, they went back to their room for their bags. Azura would be wearing her new hat, at least until they boarded the coach. Then she would carefully put it in the hat box and wear her bonnet. The coach was on time. As they boarded, they found that there was another passenger already in the coach. He was an army major returning to his regiment at Chateauroux. He would be traveling with them as far as Tours.

They were not on the road long before they started to get acquainted. The major, after finding out that William was an American, started to ask him many questions about the American Revolution; and also, what he thought about the French revolution. William answered his questions, being careful to keep his answers neutral. Azura played her role as the bashful young bride, giving short answers to any questions asked her.

Late that afternoon, Monsieur Proust arrived at the same inn that William and Azura had stayed in during their lay over in Orleans. He wasted no time in finding the inn keeper. As soon as he had the inn keeper's attention, he said, "Monsieur Inn Keeper, I am, Monsieur Proust, an agent of the Paris Committee of Public Safety."

Hearing the words, Committee of Public Safety, the inn keeper was immediately on the alert. "Yes, Monsieur Proust, how may I help you?"

Monsieur Proust could see that he had the inn keeper's full attention. Most people had this reaction when he mentioned that he was an agent of the committee. "Monsieur Inn Keeper, I am after a young couple, husband and wife, that would have passed through here two to three days ago. I don't have much of a description of them; only that the man was in his early twenties, the woman about seventeen or eighteen. They were both of average height and build."

The inn Keeper remembered the young couple that had come through and spent the night at his inn. He wondered what the Committee of Public Safety wanted them for. "What are they wanted for, Monsieur Proust?"

Monsieur Proust said, "They are wanted for questioning concerning a double homicide in Paris."

The inn keeper said, "There was a young couple through here recently. Let me get my register."

After consulting his register, he said, "Yes, there was a young couple through here recently. They were Monsieur William Hooker and his wife Monique."

"Was the man English?"

The inn keeper shook his head. "No, Monsieur Proust, the man was an American. They were on there way to Nantes, to take ship to America."

Monsieur Proust said, "When is the next coach for Nantes?"

The inn keeper said, "The next coach is in the morning. If you are staying here at the inn. We will ensure that you are ready when the coach arrives, and ensure that you have a seat in the coach."

Monsieur Proust would have been eager to continue on that night. However, he would have to spend the night at the inn and continue on in the morning. "All right, Monsieur Inn Keeper, I shall stay here for the night, and take the coach in the morning. Now, do you know who runs the Committee of Public Safety here in Orleans?"

The inn keeper nodded. "Yes, Monsieur Proust, I do."

Monsieur Proust said, "Good, then send a messenger to tell him that I would like for him to attend me here. Now, I would like to have supper."

TEN

It was early in the evening when the coach arrived at an inn in Tours. William had decided that they would stay overnight at the inn, before continuing their journey to Angers in the morning. Now that they were close to Nantes, William had decided that from Tours, they were so close to Nantes, that they might as well just keep on going until they reach their destination.

After checking on the next coach to Angers, and securing a room for the evening, they went to dinner in the common room. That evening the inn was serving roast pork, with salad, vegetables, bread and a fine wine from the Bordeaux region. It was a very enjoyable dinner. During dinner, William could hardly keep his eyes from Azura. The more time that he spent with her and got to know her, the more he realized what a wonderful young woman she was. It wasn't just the natural beauty of youth that made her so attractive, she was very smart and so far, as he had seen, had the quality's that a man would look for in a wife.

William still mourned for Monique. However, his only memory of Monique was her letters and her portrait that hung on his bedroom wall. Would he be betraying her memory if he started to show an interest in Azura. What would Monique's wishes be for him? Would she want him to go on with his life and find happiness with another woman? He was torn between his duty to Monique's memory and his growing desire for Azura. He was glad that he could take refuge in his pledge to Azura, that he would not use his position as her benefactor to take advantage of her. He knew that no matter what feelings he had for her; he would never break his pledge to her.

That evening William was the first to get in bed, as Azura took care of her needs before bed. William was in bed, with his back towards her when she started to disrobe and put on her nightgown. The light from the lamp was already turned down so low as to barely make out the objects in the room. William could easily take a peek at Azura as she was in a state of undress, but he wouldn't. he felt that it would be a violation of his pledge to her to respect her virtue.

As Azura slid in bed between the sheets, William moved as close to his edge of the bed as he could, so that there would not be any contact with her. They were both awake in the dark for a while, battling their desires, before they were able to drift off to sleep.

The next morning Azura was up first, as usual. She dressed quickly, then left for the inn's kitchen. Arriving there, she found the inn keeper's wife supervising the kitchen staff. Stepping up to the inn keeper's wife, Azura said, "Oh, Madame, may I have some hot water so that my husband can shave?"

The inn keeper's wife nodded at Azura. "Of course, Madame, I shall get it for you right away."

"Merci, Madame." Azura said.

Within minutes Azura was headed back to their room with washrag, towel and a pitcher of hot water. When she arrived back at the room, William was up and dressed, except for cravat, waistcoat and cutaway coat.

Azura placed the pitcher of hot water on the night table next to the bed. William poured some hot water into the basin on the night table. Azura then wet the washrag in hot water and washed her face, neck and hands, as William worked up a lather in his shaving mug. Azura then watched as William shaved. When William was finished shaving. He finished dressing. They then left their room to have breakfast in the common room.

Breakfast was much the same as in any outer inn. Coffee with milk and beet sugar in pitchers, fresh bread, brie, butter and this morning raspberry preserves. They loaded up their plates, poured themselves a cup of coffee, then had a seat where they had some privacy. After eating breakfast, they went back to their room for their bags; they then waited in the front courtyard of the inn for the coach. As they waited, they displayed affection for each other, as newly weds would be expected to do.

At the appointed time the coach arrived. They took their seats in the coach. There were two other passengers sharing the coach with them. They were Republican Army officers going to join their regiment in Nantes. They were both newly commissioned lieutenants. William judged their ages as no more as Azura's. He wondered what the requirements were in the Republican Army for a commission. He had heard that there were some men that had been sergeants in the King's Army before the revolution, that were now colonels or generals.

They were soon acquainted. When they found out that William was an American; they wanted to know everything he could tell them about the American Republic. As William conversed with the two passengers. He ended up telling them about the American revolution, or as most in the United States preferred to call it, the war of independence. He explained that the war in America wasn't against the Colonial governments, but to sever the ties between Britain and their former colonies, that now considered themselves as independent states.

All this time Azura acted the demure-young bride, that let her husband take the lead in discourse with other men. If she stayed out of the conversations as much as possible, she was less likely to make a blunder.

That morning, Monsieur Proust took the coach from Orleans to Tours. Now that he had names and descriptions, he had more of an idea of who he was pursuing. Now it was just a chase. He knew that they were far enough ahead of him, that he would not be able to overtake them on the road. His only chance was to get to Nantes in time to prevent them from boarding a ship and leaving France. If he can trap them in Nantes, he would eventually flush them out.

The coach carrying William and Azura arrived at an inn in Angers a little after one PM the following day. Even though they were wearied from the overnight travel, they were now close to their destination. They had decided not to spend the night in Angers, but to keep on going to Nantes. Once they were in Nantes, they would have plenty of time to rest before they took ship to America.

Finding the inn keeper, William said, "Monsieur Inn Keeper, I am Monsieur Hooker. My wife and I wish to continue on the coach to Nantes. We are anxious to get to Nantes and take ship to America."

The inn keeper looked at William, thinking that he hadn't yet heard of the most recent developments. The inn keeper said, Monsieur Hooker, no doubt you and your wife want to go to Nantes, however, I do not advise it. There is a Royalist Army of thirty to fifty thousand under command of Generalissimo Jacques Cathelineau just hours from Angers. They are on their way to attack the Republic forces in Nantes. Even if you arrived in Nantes safely; I doubt that you would have an easy time finding a ship to America."

William thought for a moment, then turned to Azura. Azura, having followed the conversation, said, "I shall abide with whatever you decide, My Husband."

Turning back to the inn keeper, William said, "We still need to take ship to America. Where would you suggest that we go?"

The inn keeper didn't even have to think about it. With war breaking out with Great Britain, all the channel ports would soon be under blockade. They would have to turn south to find an open port. They may even have to go to Spain to take ship. "Well, Monsieur Hooker, I would suggest that you head south for Bordeaux. All the channel ports will soon be under blockade by the British Royal Navy. When the word gets out that Nantes is under attack, American ships will start to use Bordeaux."

William looked to and got a nod from Azura. He then turned back to the inn keeper. "Okay, Monsieur Inn Keeper, we shall go to Bordeaux. When is the next coach going to Bordeaux?"

The inn keeper said, "The next coach going to Bordeaux leaves at eight-thirty this evening."

William realized that they could no longer afford to waste any time in getting to Bordeaux. They could no longer make any overnight layovers for rest. The next coach would leave in a little more than seven hours. They could get a few hours rest before then. "Monsieur Inn Keeper, we would like a room; and you can give us a wake-up call at seven."

They were still serving the mid-day meal in the common room of the inn, but right now sleep was more important than food. William and Azura went directly to their room. William removed only his cutaway coat, waistcoat, cravat and shoes. Azura removed only her shoes and gown, keeping on her petticoats, hose and other under garments. They quickly got into bed, being sound asleep shortly after their heads touched the pillows.

At seven that evening, there was a knock at their door. The person kept knocking until William called out that they were awake. Without delay, William and Azura got out of bed. They could have used a couple of hours more sleep; however, they were refreshed enough from what they had gotten.

As soon as Azura was dressed, she left the room and headed for the kitchen of the inn. Arriving there, she found the inn keeper's wife supervising the kitchen staff. Azura said, "Madame, Could I have some hot water, so that my husband can shave?"

The inn keeper's Wife looked at Azura. "Why, of course, Madame, I will have someone get it for you."

Azura replied, "Merci, Madame."

Minutes later she was returning to their room with a washcloth, towel and a pitcher of water. William poured some water into the basin on the night stand and started to work up a lather in his shaving mug. Azura took the washcloth, dipped it in the water and washed her face, neck and hands. She then watched William, as he lathered up and shaved.

When they were both ready, they left the room and headed to the common room. There were already a crowd in the common room having dinner. They found an empty table and ordered dinner. The Inn was serving beef stew with a green salad and fresh bread. There was a red wine to go with the meal that wasn't too bad.

After dinner they went back to their room, got their bags and went out into the front court yard of the inn to wait for the coach. When it arrived, they boarded. There were two other passengers riding with them in the coach. One was an elderly man, dressed much like a shop keeper. The other man was in his early thirties, dressed as a laborer. He had a medium size travel bag, that he was reluctant to let go of, even for a short time. He had an ambiance about him that made William feel uneasy about him. William decided that he needed to keep an eye on that one; and be ready for any unexpected occurrence.

It was early evening, when the coach arrived at the inn in tours. Monsieur Proust disembarked and went to locate the inn keeper. Finding him in the common room, Monsieur Proust said, "Monsieur Inn Keeper, I am, Monsieur Proust, an agent of the Paris Committee of Public safety. I am after a young couple that passed through here recently. They are American and traveling to Nantes to take ship to America."

The inn keeper had become apprehensive the moment that Monsieur Proust had mentioned the Committee of Public safety. The last thing he wanted was to come under the scrutiny of the Committee of public safety. "Yes, Monsieur Proust, I remember a couple that fits your description. They passed through here two days ago, on their way to Nantes."

Monsieur Proust now felt that he had a chance of catching them. They were only two days ahead of him now. If they took another stop over in Angers, then that would put him just one day behind them. He would still have a chance of trapping them in Nantes before they could leave by ship to America. "Monsieur Inn Keeper, when is the next coach to Nantes?"

The inn keeper said, "Well, Monsieur Proust, the next coach to Nantes is at nine in the morning. However, I doubt that you want to take it."

"And why is that, Monsieur Inn Keeper?" Monsieur Proust said.

The inn keeper said, "There is a Royalist Army of thirty to fifty thousand men, under the command of Generalissimo Jacques Cathelineau, moving through Angers to attack Nantes. I'm sure that the couple that you are after was warned about this when they arrived in Angers. I would be willing to put money on them heading to another port."

They can't get to Nantes. Now, where would they go? They could go to a channel port like Brest, Cherbourg, Le Havre or Calais. There they may find an American ship. Those ports are used mostly by British ships. Being that Britain is moving to war against France; they would find few ships there. Their best bet would be Bordeaux. Monsieur Proust thought.

"Monsieur Inn Keeper." Monsieur Proust said, "When is the next coach to Bordeaux?"

The inn keeper thought for a moment of the coach schedules. "Well, Monsieur Proust, there is a coach leaving at ten in the morning for Montlucon. From there you continue on through Perigueux to Bordeaux."

Monsieur Proust said, "Monsieur Inn Keeper, I want You to make sure that I have a seat on that coach in the morning; then I would like dinner and a room for the night."

"Yes, Monsieur Proust." The inn keeper said.

ELEVEN

T he man that kept a tight grip on his travel bag, even in the coach remained aloof, keeping to himself. His travel bag was always under his arm, or on the floor of the coach, behind or between his legs. William and Azura wondered what were so valuable in his travel bag that he had to keep such close watch on it.

The elderly gentleman didn't say anything at first; he just sat watching William and Azura. Finally, he addressed William, "Monsieur, are you not from America?"

William wondered how he had come to that conclusion. "You are right, Monsieur. How did you know that?"

The elderly man pointed at William's shoes. "I am a cobbler, Monsieur. I can look at a pair of shoes and tell you where they are from."

"That's really amazing." William said.

The Elderly man said, "Pardon me, Monsieur, my name is Monsieur Orville Sardon. I am from Cholet."

William shook hands with Monsieur Sardon. "I am Monsieur William Hooker." Indicating Azura, William said, "This is my wife, Monique."

Monsieur Sardon nodded to Azura. "Pleased to meet you, Madame Hooker."

"And I you, Monsieur Sardon." Azura said.

Monsieur Sardon said, "Now, Monsieur Hooker, your wife is French. I can tell that, not just from her speech, but also from her shoes."

William nodded. "That's true, Monsieur Sardon. My wife and I were married in proxy this year. I have come to France to bring her back home with me." William then told the story of how their families had been such close friends since the American Revolution, of how they had corresponded with each other since they were children, and how they had fallen in love.

Monsieur Sardon listened with acute interest. When William was finished, Monsieur Sardon said, "What a wonderful story. I wish you happiness, good fortune and many children."

At that, Azura looked at William, with a smile.

William said, "Thank you, Monsieur Sardon. My wife and I do want many children. Now, were you by chance, visiting family of your own in Angers?"

Monsieur Sardon shook his head. "No, Monsieur, I was in Angers to try to purchase leather and other supplies for my business. You can't imagine how hard it is to get good leather these days. With the threat of war, the army is taking most of it. As you know, all soldiers need boots, belts, cartridge boxes and other equipment. The army also needs saddles, bridles, halters, harness and other items for their horses. It is very difficult to get any leather at all."

William told Monsieur Sardon that he was too young to notice during the American Revolution, but he was sure that it was the same in America. William and Azura found Monsieur Sardon very likeable as a traveling companion, that made the time pass faster.

Later that morning, Monsieur Proust set out by coach from Tours for Bordeaux, by way of Montlucon, Limoges and Perigueux; to keep well clear of any area where he may encounter any Royalist soldiers. He knew that his pray would arrive in Bordeaux ahead of him. However, he felt that he could still get there in time to block them from taking a ship to America. If he could do that, he would have them trapped in the city. Then it would be only a matter of time before he captured them.

Now all that mattered was speed. Monsieur Proust knew that he wouldn't get to Bordeaux ahead of the American and his wife; that is unless they were foolish enough to make stopovers every night in route. However, seeing how quickly the port of Nantes was closed in front of them, he was sure that they would want to take ship as quickly as possible. All he had to do was get there in time to prevent them from leaving.

The coach rolled on toward Cholet. William and Azura got along well with Monsieur Sardon. The other passenger remained detached.

He spent all his time looking out the window of the coach. By now, everyone else in the coach wondered what was so valuable in that travel bag that he never lost physical contact with it.

It was early evening when the coach arrived at an inn in Cholet. This is where Monsieur Sardon left the coach. It was also where they had a change of horses and driver. William and Azura had time for a quick dinner at the inn, before the coach departed for Niort, the next leg of the trip to Bordeaux.

No new passengers boarded the coach at Cholet; so now there was only the one other man in the coach with William and Azura. The man still ignored them, continuing to stare out the window of the coach.

It was after 11:00 PM when the coach came to a barricade. The barricade was manned by four committeemen, with their caps of liberty and knives or pistols in their belts. Two National Guard soldiers, with muskets and bayonets were there for support. Two of the committeemen were holding lanterns. As soon as the coach came to a stop, the door of the coach was opened. A committeeman held out his hand to the man that was guarding the travel bag, being that he was closest to the door. "Papers, Monsieur!"

The man with the travel bag took his papers out from his coat pocket and handed them to the committeeman. "My Papers, Monsieur."

As the committeeman appeared to look over the papers, he was appraising the man's demeanor and appearance. All at once, the committeeman grabbed the other man by the wrist. "You will come with me, Monsieur!"

The man started to resist, then drew a small two barreled pistol out from under his coat and pointed it at the committeeman.

William had been on the alert for something like this. His walking cane came crashing down on the man's wrist, making him drop the pistol. The man was dragged screaming from the coach.

In all the confusion, the man was separated from his travel bag, that had been between his legs as he sat in the coach. Azura quickly maneuvered the bag with her feet to her side of the coach, hiding it under her skirts.

After they had the man under control, the committeeman turned back to William. "Thank you, citizen. That man could have hurt me."

William nodded. "He has been acting strange ever since we boarded the coach at Angers. I have been expecting something like this."

The committeeman held out his hand. "Papers, please, Monsieur."

William handed the passports and travel documents for himself and his wife to the committeeman.

After a brief inspection of the papers, the committeeman said, "You are an American, I see."

"Yes," William said, "I came to France to bring my wife back to America with me."

The committeeman returned William's papers to him. "Welcome to France, citizen. Have a pleasant journey."

After the papers of the passengers riding on the outside of the coach were checked; the coach was allowed to go on its way.

As soon as the coach was away from the barricade, Azura took the travel bag out from under her skirts. "I have wondered what was in this bag ever since we boarded the coach in Angers. Whatever it is, they would have taken it from him at the barricade. Shall we have a look in the bag, My Husband?"

William gave her a kiss on the cheek. "You are indeed a clever woman, My Wife. Yes, let us have a look."

William opened the bag and started to remove the contents. There was a change of clothing; dark-brown coat and breeches of a low-quality light-wool. Two white linen shirts, hose under wear and a shaving kit. William said, "Not much to warrant all the vigilance on this bag."

Azura said, "you're right, My Husband, there must be more."

They set to examining the bag in more detail. They soon found something sewn into the lining of the travel bag. Azura started to rip out the stitches of the lining. There were several coins of silver and gold within the lining. "Look, My Husband. He was carrying enough to get out of the country, perhaps to England; then to have enough for a good start once he was there."

Looking at the coins, William said, "Well, My Wife, they would have been taken from him anyway. We might as well have them."

They took the coins from the bag, putting them in their own travel bags. William, thinking that there could be a need for them, took the coat and breeches and put them in his own travel bag. They then extinguished the small lamp inside the coach. It was a very dark night;

so, no one seen when William threw the bag out the window of the coach as they were passing through a stand of woods.

With the coach all to themselves, they tried to get as much rest as they could. William ended up in the corner of the seat, with Azura curled up next to him, asleep with her head in his lap. William put his arm about her and dozed.

At Niort they had enough time to get something to eat. They were also able to walk about to work the stiffness out of their arms and legs. They were very tired, but they had already come half way from Angers to Bordeaux. They would be able to make it without a layover.

When the coach pulled out from Niort, there was a new passenger in the coach with them. After the coach had pulled away from the inn where he had boarded, the new passenger introduced himself. Putting forth his hand, he said, "I am, Monsieur Garlon Sartre."

William shook his hand. "A pleasure to meet you, Monsieur Sartre. I am, Monsieur William Hooker." Indicating Azura with a nod of his head towards her, he said, "This is my wife, Monique."

Monsieur Sartre nodded to Azura. "A pleasure to meet you, Madame Hooker."

Azura returned the nod. "A pleasure to meet you, Monsieur Sartre."

Monsieur Sartre said, "Are you English, Monsieur Hooker?"

William shook his head. "No, Monsieur Sartre, I am an American, from Rhode Island."

Monsieur Sartre was very interested in the fact that William was an American. There followed a long discussion on the American and French revolutions. They also discussed the differences between the American and French Republics. Monsieur Sartre was in agreement with William that the French was having to overcome the difficulties of self-government. William had to make the observation that the French people were passionate about liberty; and that he was sure that they would succeed in their revolution.

Azura stayed out of their discussion as much as possible; offering an observation or opinion only when asked. The rest of the time she professed fatigue from all the travel, staying out of the discussions. She did, however, pay attention to what was said.

William found out that Monsieur Sartre was an exporter of wine. He would buy it from the vineyards where it was produced. Then ship it to warehouses in nearby ports where he had leased space. His agents would then sell it to shippers to be exported. He was worried about the coming war with Britain. That would mean a large market lost to him. He knew that Britain had allies with the German States, and would just import more German wines.

Monsieur Sartre lived in Angouleme, but traveled often to other cities on the coast. William asked, "Monsieur Sartre, we are going to Bordeaux to take ship for America. We may be there for a week or more, before we are able to get passage on a ship bound for America. We would rather stay in someone's home, rather than at an inn. We feel that we would be more comfortable with that arrangement. Do you know of anyone in Bordeaux that rents out rooms?"

Monsieur Sartre nodded. "Yes, Monsieur Hooker, I do know of such a place in Bordeaux. The house is owned by, Madame Katia Camus. She is an elderly widow that lives alone. It is a small house, but in a quite neighborhood and she keeps it clean. I will give you directions on how to find the house, after you leave the coach at the inn in Bordeaux. He then told William how to find Madame Camus' house in Bordeaux. Azura also paid attention to the directions.

Monsieur Sartre left the coach in Angouleme. He was replaced by an elderly couple that were returning home to Bordeaux. They had been visiting their daughter and her husband in Angouleme, after the birth of their latest Grandson.

William and Azura congratulated them on the birth of their Grandson. They spoke for a while with the proud grand-parents. However, by this time, William and Azura were exhausted and just wanted to rest as much as they could.

Finally, in mid-afternoon the coach rolled into Bordeaux. After everyone's papers were checked by the committeemen at the barricade to the gates of the city. The coach went on to an inn, where everyone disembarked.

TWELVE

William and Azura wasted no time in getting away from the inn. There was still enough time left in the day; William wanted to first get a room, then visit the docks to look for a ship bound for America. He wouldn't feel secure until he had arranged passage for Azura and himself.

The instructions that they had received from Monsieur Sartre were clear; it only took them a little over a half an hour to find Madame Camus' house. It was a three-room house, similar to Azure's mother's house. As they approached it, Azura could even see the fruit trees and garden in the back, much the same as her mother's.

Stepping up to the front door, William knocked. Within a minute the door was opened by a middle-aged woman, of what William and Azura estimated to be in her mid-fifties, a little to the heavy side and graying-black hair.

William said, "Madame Camus, I am Monsieur William Hooker," Indicating Azura, he continued, "and this is my wife, Monique. A gentleman, Monsieur Sartre, that we met on the coach told us that you have a room for rent."

Madame Camus did a quick appraisal of William and Azura. They looked to her to be an upstanding young couple. With a nod, she said, "Yes, Monsieur, I do have a room for rent. I can rent it for the day, or by the week."

William said, "Well, Madame, we are here to take passage by ship to America. We don't know how long it will take us to get passage on a ship bound for America. I think that we need to rent the room by the week, with option for a second week."

Madame Camus was pleased that she would be renting the room for at least a week, perhaps two. That would be guaranteed income for up to two weeks. "Well, Monsieur, the room is available. Please, come on in and have a look at the room." She stepped back and held the door open for them.

William entered with Azura. Azura looked around; the house was much the same as her mother's house. The only difference was the furnishings and decorations. There was even a kitchen on the back of the house, the same as her mother's.

Madame Camus showed them the room that she had for rent. William and Azura took a close look at the room. It had a double bed, with a cotton-stuffed mattress. There was also a large armoire. Next to the bed was a night stand, with a porcelain basin and chamber pot. A small mirror hung on the wall above the night stand. There was also a lamp on the night stand. Looking around the room, they could see that it was clean.

William turned to, Madame Camus. "We'll take the room."

Madame Camus quoted a weekly rate. It seemed reasonable to William. After a quick conference with Azura, he accepted the room at Madame Camus' price.

After paying for the room, Madame Camus invited them to have coffee. Like Azura's mother's house, the dining table was in the central room. William and Azura sat at the table, as Madame Camus served coffee. Azura noticed that Madame Camus served coffee in bowls, the same as her mother did. She was already starting to feel at home here. Madame Camus had some milk and beet sugar to go with the coffee.

There was enough time left in the day; so, after coffee, William left for the docks to find a ship that was sailing to America. He desperately needed rest and sleep, after such a long coach ride. However, he felt that they couldn't afford to delay in finding a ship to take them away from France.

After about a forty-minute walk, William emerged from the streets of the city at the docks. Turning to the left, he started to walk along the docks. He could see that there were mostly French ships in port. Most were being unloaded or loaded with cargo. With war between France and Britain getting started, most wanted to clear harbor as quickly as possible, to avoid the blockade by the British Royal Navy, that everyone knew was coming.

After walking along the docks for about fifteen minutes, Willian spotted a two-mast topsail schooner of about ninety feet length, with the flag of the United States of America flying at the stern. As he got closer, he could make out the lettering at the stern of the ship. It read.

MARTHA WILKINS
BALTIMORE, MARYLAND

William stopped at the gangplank and called out, "Martha Wilkins, may I come aboard?"

A seaman appeared at the rail. "Why, Sir, do you wish to come aboard?"

William said, "I wish to speak to the Captain about passage for my wife and myself to the United States."

With a wave of the hand, the seaman said, "You may come aboard; I shall take you to the Captain."

William went up the gangplank, to be met by the seaman. "Come with me, Sir. I shall escort you to the Captain's cabin."

William followed the seaman into the ship, then aft to the stern cabin. The seaman knocked on the door. A voice called out from within, "Who is it?"

The seaman replied, "Captain Prescot, Sir, there is a gentleman here to see you about booking passage."

The door opened. A man at least ten years William's senior stood in the door. He was of average height and build, with a deep-lined face that showed a lifetime at sea and brown hair that was graying at the temples.

William stuck out his hand. "Captain Prescot, Sir, I am Mr. William Hooker. I wish to book passage back to the United States for my wife and myself."

Captain Prescot looked at William, then said, "We do have a passenger cabin that is still vacant. Come in and we shall talk about it."

William followed him into the cabin, where Captain Prescot indicated a chair at a small table, that was bolted to the deck. William sat in the chair, the Captain sitting in another chair across the table from him.

When they both were seated, Captain Prescot begin, "So, Mr. Hooker, you want to book passage with me; where are you from in the United States?"

William said, "I am from Newport, Rhode Island, Captain."

Captain Prescot said, "We are bound for Baltimore. Why don't you wait for a ship bound for say New York or Boston, it would be much more convenient for you."

William said, "We were headed for Nantes to take ship, when it came under siege by a Royalist army. We now feel that the political situation is so unstable, that we must leave as quickly as possible, while we can."

Captain Prescot nodded. "Yes, I understand. With all the turmoil, you can't foresee from one day to the next what is going to happen. I would be glad to take you and your wife as passengers."

William was thrilled that they had a ship to take them home. The next few minutes were spent settling the price for passage. William then gave Captain Prescot a deposit to reserve the cabin.

After the price of passage had been agreed on; and a deposit put down to reserve the cabin, Captain Prescot said, "Well, Mr. Hooker, perhaps you have noticed that we have just began to unload our cargo. After we devest ourselves of this cargo; we shall then take on a new cargo. We will then have to re-provision and refill our water casks. You and your wife should board the ship in three days, in the afternoon. By then, everything should be taken care of. Any earlier and you would just be in the way."

William nodded. "Yes, Captain, three days from now, in the afternoon. My wife and I shall be here with our bags, ready to go."

William shook hands with Captain Prescot. He then left the ship to return to Madame Camus' house.

Arriving back at Madame Camus' house, William found Azura in the kitchen with Madame Camus, preparing dinner. While William had been out, Azura had gone to the market with Madame Camus, to shop for dinner.

William took Azura in his arms and kissed her. "Good news, My Wife, I have booked passage for us to America. We will be sailing on the Baltimore schooner, Martha Wilkins. Captain Prescot, the ship's captain, doesn't want us to board now; we would just be in the way, while they unload and load cargo, then provision for sea. We are to board three days from now."

Azura hugged William. "Oh, that's wonderful, My Husband, I can hardly wait. Is the ship taking us to Newport, Rhode Island?"

William shook his head. "No, My Wife, the ship is going to Baltimore. From there, we can take another ship to Newport, or we can go by coach."

Azura said, "I don't want anymore long coach rides, My Husband; let us go by ship."

William chuckled, then kissed Azura again. All right then, My Wife, no more coach rides."

That evening they had lamb chops for dinner. Azura had given Madame Camus money to get this special treat for them. Azura had also gotten raspberry tarts at the bakery for dessert.

William and Azura went to bed that evening, feeling secure that they had a ship that would take them away from danger, to America.

Late that night, the coach carrying Monsieur Proust, passed through the city gates of Bordeaux. After identifying himself to the committeemen on the barricade as an agent of the Paris Committee of Public Safety, Monsieur Proust inquired if an American couple had recently arrived in Bordeaux.

The committeeman at the barricade shook his head. "We really don't know, Monsieur Proust. We have been on duty for less than two hours. No Americans, that we know of, has passed through the barricade."

Monsieur Proust continued on through the barricade. As soon as he arrived at the inn; he sought out the inn keeper. He found the inn keeper in the common room. "Monsieur Inn Keeper," he said, "I am, Monsieur Proust, an agent of the Paris Committee of public Safety. Do you know the head of the Committee of Public safety here in Bordeaux?"

At the mention of the committee of Public Safety, the inn keeper started to break out in a nervous sweat. "Yes, Monsieur Proust, I do know the leader of the local Committee of Public Safety."

"Good," Monsieur Proust said with a smile. "If you would send a runner to inform him that I am here; and that I request his presents here at the inn on urgent committee business."

The inn keeper nodded. "Yes, Monsieur Proust, it shall be done."

Monsieur Proust said, "Good, now I would like dinner and a room for the night."

An hour later, Monsieur Proust was having a meeting with Monsieur Carrel, the head of the committee of Public Safety in Bordeaux, in his room at the inn. They were sitting across from each other, at a small table in the room. Monsieur Proust said, "Thank you for coming, Monsieur Carrel. I am after a young American couple that might have come to Bordeaux to take ship for America. They are wanted for questioning, concerning a double homicide in Paris. They are Monsieur William and Madame Monique Hooker. I need to know if they passed through any of the barricades into Bordeaux."

Monsieur Carrel, rested his chin in the cup of his hand, as he thought. He then looked up. "Monsieur Proust, I can have the committeemen at the barricades questioned about rather or not this couple is in Bordeaux. However, I doubt that you would get any information. There are a lot of people moving in and out of the city each day. They check all travel documents, but most of the committeemen on the barricades can't read: they look for the official stamps and seals on the documents. They also look at the peoples faces and hands."

Monsieur Proust said, "Then, why don't you have people on the barricades that can read?"

Monsieur Carrel shrugged. "It's the best we can do. Educated men have jobs to go to. We have to make do with who ever we can get. It is mostly the unemployed that volunteers for duty on the barricades for a small wage."

Monsieur Proust knew that he could do nothing about the quality of the personnel manning the barricades. Any man with a good education was able to easily find better employment than the barricades. At least he had been able to get the names of the two that he was after, from the inn keepers where they stayed for the night. He said, "Well, Monsieur Carrel, at least I have their names. They are Monsieur William and Madame Monique Hooker; they are traveling on American passports. If they have not arrived in Bordeaux yet, we can catch them at the barricades. If they are here, we can prevent them from boarding a ship. I want committeemen and National Guard patrols on the docks. They are to check the papers of anyone who approaches the ships tied up at the docks. You will check all the inns, hotels and boarding houses near the docks, to see if they have taken a room. I want these patrols started now."

Monsieur Carrel nodded. "Yes, Monsieur Proust, I shall take care of it now." He then left to carry out his orders.

THIRTEEN

Azura awoke first in the morning. She got out of bed, dressed and went into the kitchen. Madame Camus was already in the kitchen, getting ready to fix breakfast. Azura said, "Madame Camus, May I have some hot water, so that my husband might shave?"

Madame Camus said, "Of course, Madame Hooker. The stove is already heated, so it won't take long to heat the water."

Madame Camus took a dipper and filled a pan with water, from a small cask next to the stove and put it on the stove to heat.

When the water was hot enough, Azura carried it, along with a washrag and towel, back to their bedroom. William was out of bed and dressed in shirt, breeches, hose and shoes. She poured the hot water into the basin on the night stand. While William got out his shaving kit and started to make lather in his shaving mug; Azura dipped the washrag into the hot water, then washed her face, neck and hands. She then watched William, as he shaved. Azura never got tired of watching William shave. It was a manly ritual, that she had never witnessed before she met William.

When William had finished shaving, they went out to the kitchen, Madame Camus had the coffee ready. Madame Camus had gone to a nearby bakery early that morning to buy bread. The milkman was also by early. Madam Camus purchased two liters of milk from him. Azura noticed that Madame Camus served coffee in bowls, instead of cups, the same as her mother did. There was milk and beet sugar for the coffee. To go with the coffee, was the bread, butter, home made apricot preserves and brie.

During breakfast, they talked of what they were going to do that day. Azura would be helping Madame Camus with cleaning the house:

then helping her with the shopping. Madame Camus reminded Azura of her mother: and they had become friends right away. She wasn't just going to lay about, while Madame Camus did all the work, just because they had paid for the lodging. She wanted to help, to have something to do. William planned to visit the docks, to see the ship that they were to take. He would then do some work in the garden for Madame Camus that afternoon.

At about 10:00 AM, William left for the docks. He went by a more or less direct route to the dock where the ship that they were to take to America was tied up. As he came to the intersection of the last street before the docks, he saw a patrol of committeemen and National Guard soldiers. As he watched, they stopped a man approaching one of the ships, to check his papers.

William back tracked one street, then moved three streets over to the left. He then approached the docks again. Coming up into the shadow of a corner building; William looked up and down the docks. There were other patrols of committeemen and National Guard soldiers patrolling the docks. William had seen enough, he returned to Madame Camus' house.

Azura helped Madame Camus with the house work, before they departed for the market, about one hour after William had departed to the docks. Madame Camus grew most of the vegetables that she needed for her own use. What she didn't use, she sold to customers that she had acquired over the years. She also raised chickens and rabbits. She kept enough for her own needs; selling the surplus rabbits, chickens and eggs. What she had to buy at the market was meat, fish, baked goods, dairy products and other items in small quantities.

After Madame Camus purchased some sausage for the evening meal; they went to the bakery. At the bakery, Madame Camus purchased bread. Azura then purchased cherry tarts for everyone to have for dessert that evening.

When they arrived back home, they found that William had returned from the docks. Looking at William's face, Azura felt that there was something wrong. Azura would like to ask him what was wrong, but not here or now. They would have to wait until they had more privacy.

After lunch, William offered to turn the ground in the garden, where Madame Camus wanted to plant some vegetables. He changed into the clothes that he had taken from the travel bag on the coach, they were a little large for him, making him look unkept. However, at least they would be useful for gardening.

As William worked to turn the soil, Azura came out to join him. William hadn't said anything yet, but she sensed that something was wrong. "What is it, My Husband?" Azura said, "You have a worried look that concerns me."

William had seen Madame Camus go into the house, so he could speak to Azura without being over heard. "Well, My Wife, when I arrived at the docks this morning, I saw a patrol of committeemen and National Guard soldiers patrolling the docks. They were stopping everyone that approached a ship and checked their papers. I looked elsewhere along the docks and saw other patrols doing the same."

Azura felt a stab of cold, like a blade of ice. They didn't have the proof yet, but Azura was sure that the patrols were looking for them. "Oh, My Husband, do you think that they are looking for us."

William shook his head, as he continued to turn the soil. "Oh, My Wife, I don't know. However, we would be fools not to suspect that they are looking for us. For sure, if they are looking for a young couple, we should not be seen together. I shall go on my own to the docks to try and find out who they are looking for. Also, we should dress differently that as we dressed during our coach trip from Paris to here." That would be easy enough. William had the clothing that he was now wearing. Azura had her own gowns in her travel bag.

Azura said, "My Husband, do you think that there might be a way to get past the patrols to the ship?"

William shook his head. "I doubt so, My Wife. If they are looking for someone, they are not likely to give up so soon. For sure, we can't approach the ship openly, least we be stopped and asked to show our papers." William could see the fear start to come to her eyes. Her safety and wellbeing had become paramount to him. He put a hand to her shoulder. "Have no doubt, My Wife, that if possible, I shall find a way to get on that ship; and that I shall never leave you behind."

Azura was encouraged by William's confidence. She kissed him on the cheek. "Thank you, My Husband. I am sure that you shall find a way." She turned to walk back to the house.

Madam Camus had been watching them from the kitchen. She could see from their demeanor that they were concerned about something. She wondered what it was, however, it wasn't her business. She was sure that if they needed her advice or help, they would ask for it.

That evening at dinner, there was little talk about the ship that they were to sail on for America. Madame Camus had begun to wonder if there was some problem with them taking passage on the ship. Finally, she said, "Monsieur Hooker, I since you and Madame are worried about something. Perhaps I could be of some help."

William looked at Madame Camus. "It's really nothing, just a minor problem. Nothing that we can't take care of."

Madame Camus dropped the subject. She had offered her assistance. If they needed her help, they would ask.

Monsieur Proust was having a meeting with Monsieur Carrel, the head of the Committee for Public Safety in Bordeaux, Monsieur Proust said "Monsieur Carrel, have all the inns, hotels and boarding houses in the city been checked for this couple, Monsieur William and Madame Monique Hooker?"

Monsieur Carrel nodded. "Yes, Monsieur Proust, we have checked all places of lodging in the city. So far, we have not come up with any couple that matches their description, under any name." Monsieur Carrel was starting to wonder it this couple that Monsieur Proust was after had come to Bordeaux. After all, there were many other ports that they could have gone to.

Monsieur Proust wasn't satisfied with Monsieur Carrel's search of the places in the city that took boarders. He knew that they were here. They must be staying in a private home, that wasn't registered as a boarding house. He was sure that they were somewhere in the city. If they try to leave the city, they will be arrested. With the patrols on the docks, they can't get close to a ship without being arrested. There is no where they can go. Eventually he will have them. He said, "Well, Monsieur Carrel, even if we haven't found them yet, I'm sure that they are here in Bordeaux. This was the most logical place that they could have come, when they couldn't get to Nantes. We just have to keep looking until we find them."

"Yes, Monsieur Proust, we shall do that." Monsieur Carrel said. He would like to call all this off. It was draining resources from other tasks that he had to take care of. However, Monsieur Proust was from the Paris Committee of Public Safety. He would have to go along for a while, before he could request that Monsieur Proust be recalled.

The next morning after breakfast, William got dressed to go to the docks. He had decided that for now he would wear the clothing that he had taken from the other man's travel bag in the coach, so as to look like just another working man. To also alter his appearance, he would not shave for now. Azura didn't like that. She preferred to see him clean shaven. However, she would say nothing and go along with it.

Leaving the house, William walked to the docks. As he drew near the last intersection before the docks, he paused in the shadow of the corner building to survey the docks. A quick look up and down the docks confirmed that the patrols were still there. He looked at the schooner Martha Wilkins. Their cargo had now been unloaded. Wagons had started to arrive at the dock with a new cargo for the ship. Stevedores had started to assemble on the dock to load the cargo onto the ship.

William watched the activity around the ship for a couple of minutes, then turned away and started to walk down the street that ran next to the river and docks. He soon came to a middle-aged woman, perhaps a couple of years younger than his mother, who was selling bonnets rouge. They were being worn by a good many people on the streets. He purchased two bonnets rouge from the woman, one for Azura and one for himself. He figured that they would help him and Azura blend in better with the local crowd.

He next stopped at a café and took a seat at a sidewalk table and ordered a glass of wine. As he slowly sipped his wine, he watched the activity about the docks. He made sure not to stare at any one thing for more than a few seconds. Or to focus his attention mostly on the schooner, Martha Wilkins. As he glanced here and there along the docks, he noticed that the patrols were still active in stopping and checking people's papers. William was now fairly sure that they were looking for Azura and himself.

After finishing his wine, William started back to Madame Camus' house. On the way, he stopped at a wine shop to purchase two bottles of wine for Madame Camus, so that there would be enough wine for their meals. He knew that most people would feel that by paying for their board, everything should be included. He felt that Madame

Camus had treated them well so far, and wanted to show her their appreciation.

While William was at the docks, Azura had first helped Madame Camus clean the house. They then went to the market to do the daily shopping. At the market, Azura insisted in purchasing a large carp for the evening meal. After Madame Camus had gotten the rest of what she needed, they started back to the house.

William was there when they arrived from the market. Madame Camus could see that he was concerned about something. She was curious about what it was, however, it was their business. If they needed her advice or help, they could ask for it.

That night in bed, William couldn't sleep right away. He was worried if they would be able to get aboard the ship or not before it sailed. He knew that if it came to it, he would stand a better chance of getting away from France alone, than with Azura. However, he knew that he could never do that, not just because he had given his word to her that he would not abandon her to save himself, but that he now loved her. For better or for worse their lives were permanently joined.

Azura lay beside him, also having a hard time sleeping. She felt the need to be embraced by William, to feel secure in his arms. However, they had to continue to sleep back to back in the bed. Willian's honor required that he not take advantage of her. So even though they were in the same bed, there should be no direct contact with each other. Azura knew that William had his honor to inhibit his desires. However, in her case, there were no such inhibitions. She desired to be held in his arms; to feel the security of his embrace. She knew that if he wanted to have her, that she would welcome him.

The next day, William returned to the proximity of the docks. He took care to take a different route, and not to frequent the same establishments, as he took his leisure. He observed that the patrols were still active in the area of the docks. He felt a little silly sitting at a sidewalk table in front of a café wearing his bonnet rouge as he sipped his wine, but it helped to blend in with the other men on the street.

As he sat there, one wild scheme after the other raced through his head. Perhaps there could be a commotion, a fire, or some other distraction to draw the patrols away from the Martha Wilkins long enough for Azure and himself to board. In the end William had to admit that they were just wishful thinking.

On the last day before the sailing of the Martha Wilkins, William again returned to the docks. Seeing the patrols, he knew that they would never get the chance to board the Martha Wilkins. Dejected, William returned to Madame Camus' house. He would have to tell Azura that they wouldn't be sailing on the Martha Wilkins.

FOURTEEN

Madame Camus had become concerned about her boarders. There was a ship that they were to have sailed on this morning. However, the ship had departed and they had not gone with it. She had begun to sense that there was more going on with this young couple than she was being told. She had started to like them, but if there were any secret that they were keeping from her that could cause a problem for her, she needed to know.

She didn't want to confront them together. They would just come up with a story and stick to it. She decided that she would confront Madame Hooker tomorrow, after her husband leaves for the docks.

That evening at dinner. The conversation was about anything else, except the ships or docks. That was all right with Madame Camus, she could see that despite the fact they were trying to hide it, they were worried about something.

After dinner, William and Azura went for a walk. Being almost alone on the residential streets, they had the time to talk in privacy. During the walk, they talked about what they should do if the patrols continued. Azura could not come up with any ideas, at least none that she felt had a chance. Finally, she suggested, "What if we could find a way out of Bordeaux? Then perhaps we could make it to Spain and get a ship there."

William shook his head. "No, that wouldn't work. Even if we could get out of Bordeaux, we wouldn't get far. If they are looking for us, they will be looking for us at every barricade from here to the Spanish frontier. It's best that we remain here where we can hide amongst the population of the city. When they don't find us, they will eventually have to call the patrols off. Then we should be able to get a ship."

Azura knew that if she wasn't with him, that he would have a much better chance of getting away. Any other man that she had ever known, would have abandoned her by now to save themselves. She really couldn't blame William if he left her behind. Afterall, just a few days ago they had been strangers. He really didn't owe her any more than he had already done for her. Only his since of honor was holding him to her. If he is able to get her safely out of France; she shall owe him more than she could ever pay.

The next day, William left after breakfast for the docks. He took another way, so that no one would notice that he had a routine. He would not only vary the route, but also the time. Tomorrow, he would wait until after Azura and Madame Camus left for the market.

Arriving at the docks, he looked for, but could see no American ships. There were also no English ships, being that war with England had just started. Most of the ships in port were French. Few French ships were now taking on cargos; being that the English would soon have a blockade in place. Even if there were a French ship leaving. He doubted it they could get out on it. He had a coffee at a sidewalk café, then went to a bakery to get some peach tarts for dinner that evening.

After doing the cleaning, Madame Camus said to Azura, "Well, Madame Hooker, why don't we have a coffee before we go shopping?"

With a smile, Azura said, "That's all right with me."

After the coffee was made, and they were sitting at the table, Madame Camus said, "Madame Hooker, I can't help but notice that you and your husband are worried about something. I also know that you and your husband had booked passage on a ship, and were supposed to have left on it. Now the ship is gone and you are still here. Now I don't know what's going on, or what problems you might have. I just don't want any trouble. Now, if you have anything you want to tell me, I'm ready to listen."

Azura took a sip of coffee from her bowl, then sat it back down on the table. She just looked into the bowl for a minute, deciding on what to tell Madame Camus. She finally came to the conclusion that only the truth would do. Azura looked up at Madame Camus and said, "It's a long story. It starts in Paris. However, I first have an admission to say to you. William and I are not husband and wife. I am Mademoiselle Azura Gauzet. I was in the service of Madame Marie Jeanne Du Barry. At first, I was just a domestic. You know, making the beds, cleaning, that sort of thing. Later, when I learned to speak Spanish, Italian and English, Madame Du Barry used me to gather information from gentlemen and ladies at the palace."

Madame Camus nodded that she understood so far. Azura continued, "Well, when Madame Du Barry was arrested, I left the palace and went back home. I just wanted to be done with it and move on with my life. Then one night, committeemen came to our home to arrest me as a royalist sympathizer. I was able to get away and make it to Paris. Mother had told me to go to Paris and try to get papers so that I could make it to a port and get away to England.

"It was night when I got to Paris, And I was looking for a place to stay; when two men jumped out of an alleyway and seized me. They said that they were going to turn me in to the Committee of Public Safety, but first they were going to rape me. When they grabbed me and started to grope me, I screamed.

"William happened to be close by when I screamed. Most people would have been reluctant to get involved, especially when the odds were two to one against them. William, however, rushed to my aid without hesitation. He struck one man with his cane, and the man went down mortally injured. The second man was a giant of a man; and quickly had William on the pavement, trying to crush the life from him. Seeing the knife that the other man had dropped; I took it and struck him, killing him.

"Oh, Madame, it was horrible. I have never killed a man before. However, I was in such a state of terror and panic that I couldn't help myself."

Madame Camus reached out and patted Azura's hand. She understood that it had been a frightful experience for Azura. If she had been in Azura's place, she would have likely done the same.

Oh, Mademoiselle, I understand that it was a frightful experience for you. Being in your place, I would have most likely done the same. Those two men were criminals, for what they were about to do to you. You did what you had to do. Now, what happened after that?"

Azura took a deep breath to calm herself, then continued, "Well, Madame, William then took me to his room where he was staying. Having rescued me, he felt responsible for me. He was on his way back home. He had come to France to get his bride whom he had married in proxy. However, before he arrived, she had died of tetanus. He had the passports and travel documents for the both of them, so he offered to take me with him to America. There was, however, the stipulation that I had to pose as his wife Monique. I was willing until he said that to make our pretense convincing, we would even have to share the same bed when staying overnight at the inns where we stopped. At first, I balked at the idea; being a virgin, I had never been in bed with any man before. He said that it was necessary, saying that any maid could see how many people slept in a bed. He then gave me his word of honor that he would not use his position as my protector to take advantage of me. That he would defend my virtue as well as my person against all threats. That he would not abandon me; and as long as I was with him, no harm shall come to me. So far he has kept his word."

Madame Camus was finding Azura's story very interesting. She could not find any blame in Azura or William for what they had done. As for Azura being wanted by the Committee of Public Safety, she knew that a lot of the accusations were just one person trying to get revenge for a slight, real or imagined. She was also enthralled by the tale of William's chivalry. Such men were rare. She made her decision. "Mademoiselle, I shall keep yours and William's secret. I shall also help you however I can."

Tears begin to roll down Azura's cheeks. She grabbed and squeezed Madame Camus' hand. "Oh, thank you, Madame Camus; we shall be no trouble for you."

Madame Camus smiled. "I am curious about one thing, Mademoiselle. Sleeping in the same bed, how do you manage to maintain your virtue?"

Azura took a moment, then looked at Madame Camus. "Well, Madame, first of all, we sleep back to back. Even so, from time to time in the night we touch. As time has gone by, I have grown from being wary of him, to now having a desire for him. If he wanted me, I would willingly accept him. I now dream of having him embracing me in his arms, and kissing me with passion. I even wonder how it would feel to have him inside me."

Madame Camus was enjoying this. "Mademoiselle, how do you and William resist each other in the bed?"

Azura said, "Well, Madame, William has his word of honor to help him resist his urges. As for me, there is no such inhibition.

Every time his body touches me, I shiver with desire and want him desperately. It is very hard Madame."

Madame Camus could imagine what Azura was going through, by hers and William's restraint. Finally, she said, "Well, Madame Hooker, are you ready to go shopping?"

Starting to rise from the table, Azura said, "Yes, Madame Camus."

When William got back to the house, Azura and Madame Camus were still out shopping. He busied himself making repairs to the rabbit hutch and the door to the tool shed for Madame Camus. After that, he went to an open lot close by, that Madame Camus had said that he could cut fodder for the rabbits.

At the market, Madame Camus purchased some lamb for stew. Azura then purchased some goose liver pate. At the bakery, Madame Camus got enough bread for the evening meal. Azura bought butter croissants.

Madame Camus said, "Madame Hooker, if you keep buying these extra treats; I shall have to let out the seams of my clothing."

Azura laughed. "Oh, Madame Camus, I don't mean to cause you any in convenience. I just like to show my appreciation to you."

Madame Camus smiled. "Your company is appreciation enough for me, Madame Hooker."

When they got back home. William had just returned from cutting fodder for the rabbits. Madame Camus built up the fire in the stove, then put water on for coffee.

When they were all seated at the table with their coffee. Azura said to William. "My Husband, Madame Camus and I had a long talk this morning." William looked at her, wondering what she was coming to. She continued, "She had sensed that there was some secret that we were keeping from her. I told her of our true relationship with each other."

William just sat there with a surprised look on his face. He opened his mouth, but couldn't find the words to say.

Madame Camus then said, "Yes, Mademoiselle Gauzet told me everything about why you two are posing as husband and wife. I know of the trouble in Paris. I can find no blame for you for what happened in Paris. As I see it, you were just defending yourselves. I have agreed to keep your secret. If there is any way that I can help, just ask."

Finally, William gave Madame Camus a nod. "Thank you, Madame Camus. I assure you that we will cause you no trouble. They have patrols of committeemen and National Guard soldiers patrolling the docks now. However, they can't keep it up forever. Eventually we will be able to get a ship for America." Even as he said the words, he wondered just how much he really believed them. Could he and Azura really out last the authorities.

That evening at dinner, they talked about the patrols on the docks, and how they might get by them. William said, "I have thought about causing a diversion, like a fire, or some other disturbance. However, for that we would have to have help. Other than that, the only other way is to approach the ships from the river."

Madame Camus thought for a moment. "If it would be of any help; I know of some boats that are kept up river from the docks a short way. There are some small docks where they are kept. The boats are quite small and some really old. They are used to fish the river for carp and other fish."

William said, "Can you tell me where they are kept, Madame Camus?"

Madame Camus said, "I shall make you a map and instructions on how to find the docks where they are kept."

William nodded. "Thank you, Madame Camus."

That evening, when they went to bed, William felt that they had a better chance than they had had so far to get out of France. He was now even more determined to find a ship and get Azura to safety.

FIFTEEN

For the next four days, William visited the docks to see if any American ships had made port. He never took the same route and varied his time. He would always stop off at a café, wine shop, or other business establishment where he could spend a few minutes, while he could covertly observe the activity on the docks; and what new ship arrivals were tied up at the docks.

Each day he had to report to Azura, that no American ships had made port. They were sure to come eventually; with Nantes under siege, Bordeaux was the next best port of call for American ships.

William had also taken the time to follow Madame Camus' instructions and map to check out the small boats that were tied up to small docks a little way up river from the commercial docks of the city. The boats were well away from any homes or business establishments; making it easy to approach at night undetected. Seeing the boats, he could understand why they could be left unguarded. They were mostly old skiffs, punts and other small work boats that were used to maintain the ships hulls while in port. When they were at the end of there useful life, they were sold for a small price.

William walked along the small docks, inspecting the boats. Some of the docks were nothing more than two wide planks run out over the water from the river bank, and supported by two post driven into the riverbed. The boats, being old, were in various states of disrepair. Some were still moderately safe; others were so badly maintained, that he wouldn't trust them more than fifty feet from the riverbank. He finally identified a few that would suit his needs.

Over the next five days, three American ships arrived in Bordeaux. At last, American ships were starting to divert from Nantes to Bordeaux in large numbers. William visited the docks everyday to check on the ships in port. He wanted desperately to make contact with one of the ships, and find some way to get himself and Azura aboard, to no avail. There were always patrols on the docks, especially near the American ships.

Monsieur Proust paced the floor before the head of the Bordeaux Committee of Public Safety. He was frustrated that all their efforts so far had shown no results. "Monsieur Carrel, what do you have to report? Have you got any leads as to the American couple that we are looking for?"

Monsieur Carrel had to shake his head in resignation. "No, Monsieur Proust, we have no information on them as to rather or not they are in the city. No one has reported seeing a young couple such as has been described. There is no one registered in any hotel, inn, or boarding house under the name of William or Monique Hooker. I can't even be sure that they are in Bordeaux."

Monsieur Proust shook his fist in the air in rage. "They must be here! This the most logical place for them to come to get an American ship! You are just not looking hard enough!"

Monsieur Carrel, was straining to keep his temper in check. They were working hard to find this American couple. He was doing everything he could with the men he had. "Monsieur Proust, we are doing the best we can. With the barricades and the dock patrols, our resources are stretched thin. I don't know how much longer we can keep these patrols up."

Monsieur Proust turned to Monsieur Carrel. "Your people are just lazy, Monsieur Carrel. You need to motivate your people; make them work harder."

All that Monsieur Carrel could say was, "Yes, Monsieur Proust, I shall do my best to inspire my men. If that American couple are here in Bordeaux, we shall find them."

Monsieur Proust turned on his heel and left the room.

Monsieur Carrel watched him go. He could see that catching this American couple had become an obsession to Monsieur Proust. He had to comply for now. He would give it another week to ten days; then he would write a letter to the Paris Committee of Public Safety, asking that Monsieur Proust be recalled.

The next morning after breakfast, William did some work in the garden for Madame Camus. Azura, as usual, helped Madam Camus with the house cleaning. Madame Camus and Azura then went shopping, to get what was needed for the day.

They first stopped at the fish market. There Azura purchased an eel for dinner. It would be really good baked, with a lemon-butter sauce. From the fish market, they went to buy some fruit and vegetables that Madame Camus didn't grow in her own garden. They then stopped at the bakery for bread. While there, Azura purchased strawberry tarts for dinner.

When they arrived back home, William had completed the work in the garden. Madame Camus stoked the fire in the stove, then put on water for coffee. In a few minutes the coffee was ready. They all sat at the table and had lunch.

After lunch, William decided that he had let his beard grow enough. He would shave it. Being clean shaven, he would present a fresh-new look, other that the unkept person with the several days growth of beard. That way, he would be altering his appearance a little. Azura got hot water for him, and watched him shave.

After he finished shaving, she kissed him on the cheek. "Now, that's what I like." She said.

William then got ready to go to the docks. As usual, he wore his bonnet rouge. When at first, he had started wearing it, Azura thought it had made him look silly. Now she was used to seeing him in it. She had the bonnet rouge that he had gotten for her. However, since Madame Camus never wore one, she never wore it.

William left for the docks. He took what appeared to be a rambling route to the docks. He had taken to varying his rout each day, so that he would walk a portion of the route from Madame Camus' house to where the boats were. That way, he would learn the route well. He even learned of the houses where they had dogs in the yard, that would bark as a person walked by. He didn't want to leave anything to chance.

Coming to the docks, he stopped as usual, in the shadow of the corner building to get an idea of what new ships that had made port. He would also look to see where the patrols were. After having his look, he begins to stroll along the road, seeming to be paying attention to the shops, as he took account of what was happening on the docks. He noticed that another American ship had made port today.

After walking four blocks along the docks, William stopped at a sidewalk café. He sat at a table and ordered coffee. As he slowly drank his coffee, he observed what was happening on the docks. There was still no way that he could see to get to any of the ships without being stopped by one of the patrols to have his and Azura's papers checked.

From the café, he started to return to Madame Camus' house. On the way he stopped at a wine shop to purchase two bottles of wine. He didn't know what they would be having for dinner, so he got a bottle of red and a bottle of white.

That evening they had the eel. Eel wasn't a dish that William was used to. However, he found it to be very tasty. He didn't know much about eel. He didn't even know if this one came from the river, or the Bay of Biscay; although he knew that there were both fresh and salt water eels. Wait until they get to Newport. He was sure that Azura would love lobster with butter.

That evening William went to bed, determined to find a way to get on a ship. He knew that if it was just himself, that he would have a better chance. However, there was no way that he would abandon Azura to fend for herself. It was now more than just a pledge to her that motivated him; he now had a genuine affection for her. He wanted to always be her protector.

The next morning at breakfast, William was distracted by thought, as he evaluated in his mind first one then another scheme to get aboard a ship. In the end, he had to admit that most ideas were based mostly on wishful thinking, having little chance for success. He figured that he and Azura could get aboard a ship in the night, by approaching it from the river in a small boat. However, he would have to be certain that once reaching the ship, that he and Azura would be taken aboard. There was always the chance that the captain, fearing that giving refuge to them, would put him and his crew in jeopardy, would turn them away.

Later, as William was in their bedroom getting ready to go to the docks, Azura entered. "William," she said, "You are worried that we might not be able to get on a ship and leave France together?"

William looked at her for a moment, then nodded. "Yes, I am worried. We could take one of the boats at night and get to a ship from the river. However, we couldn't be sure ahead of time if they would take us aboard."

Azura looked down at the floor, then back up to William. "If you were alone, would you have a better chance of being taken aboard?"

William, knowing that he would have a better chance alone, nodded. "Yes, being an American citizen, my chances would be better. A lot of Ship Masters would not be willing to chance giving refuge to a French citizen."

Looking into William's eyes, Azura said, "Oh, William, you have done enough for me already. If you have the chance, save yourself. I will be safe enough now."

William reached out and took her by the shoulders. "Azura, I gave you my solemn oath that I would shield you from all harm and see that you reached safe haven. I will never leave you to fend for yourself, in favor of my own wellbeing. There will be no further talk about you being left behind."

Azura fell into William's arms. "Oh, William, I am so frightened. Well we ever be able to get away to safety in America?"

William kissed her with passion. "Take heart, Azura, as long as we don't give up, we are not beaten."

Later, as William walked to the docks, he thought of Azura. He knew that she was frightened, that she worried that the committeemen would find them. Even so she had been willing to release him of his obligation to her, so that he could save himself. She would sacrifice herself in favor of his safety. He knew that he could not let her down. He had to find a way to get them both on a ship for America.

Arriving at the last intersection before the docks; William stood in the shadow of the corner building for a couple of minutes to observe if there were any changes. There had been some departures early this morning. Looking up and down river, he couldn't see any new arrivals. Since he had come to the up river end of the docks today, he would stroll down river.

After walking five blocks, he could ascertain that no new American ships had arrived. He stopped at a sidewalk café, where he took a table and ordered a glass of wine. As he sipped his wine, he glanced about. As far as he could see, there were no changes along the docks. The patrols were still active.

Arriving back at Madame Camus' house, he wasn't looking forward to telling Azura that no new American ships had made port.

He was beginning to become discouraged. Ship after ship had entered Bordeaux and departed, but they were still there. Would there ever be a chance for them to get away.

Azura had seen him coming down the street, and had met him at the door. She could see right away that he was in a disheartened mood. "She Embraced him as soon as he came through the door, kissing him on the lips with Vigor. "Welcome home, My Husband, what say that you have a seat at the table, while I make coffee for us."

William took a seat at the table. No matter how down he was, Azura had a way of lifting his spirits. He had started to feel a need for her. He now looked forward to waking up each morning to see her lovely face.

It was but a few minutes until everyone was sitting at the table, drinking coffee from bowls. Madame Camus had gotten to know William and Azura quite well, and was concerned that rather or not they could get safely away to America. Finally, William said, "Everything is still the same. No new American Ships have arrived. I shall try again tomorrow

The next morning, after breakfast, William Did some garden work for Madame Camus, before he left for the docks. He took a route that brought him to the intersection just one block up river from the café where he had stopped for wine the day before. After observing the docks for a couple of minutes; He started to walk up river.

He had walked up river for a little more than two blocks, when he caught sight of a three-mast topsail schooner up ahead. There was something about the mast, yards and rigging that interested him. As he got closer, He could see that it was a big schooner, well over a hundred foot long. The colors of the paint on the masts, yards and hull looked familiar. Then he caught sight of the stern of the ship and froze in his tracks. The name on the stern of the ship, in gilded letters read.

YANKEE ENDEAVOR
NEWPORT, RHODE ISLAND

He could hardly believe it. The Yankee Endeavor here in Bordeaux. It was all he could do to contain his excitement. He turned around and took the next corner, to leave the docks to go back to Madame Camus' house. This was news that he had to tell Azura.

SIXTEEN

Azura was looking out the window; and saw William coming up the road. She could tell right away that there was a change in him. He was striding quickly, with a spring in his step. He was also smiling.

Azura met him at the door. "What is it, My Husband?'

Willian embraced her and kissed her with ardor. When the kiss had ended, he said, "I have wonderful news, My Wife; I saw a ship in port today. It is the Yankee Endeavor."

Azura, looking at him, said, "What's so special about this ship, the Yankee Endeavor?"

William said, "My father is part owner, along with my Uncle Adam and one other gentleman in Newport, Rhode Island. Also, My Uncle Adam is the Captain of the Yankee Endeavor. All we have to do is get along side of the ship and they will take us aboard. I'm sure of it."

By now Azura was just as excited as William. Herring William and Azura by the front door, Madame Camus came out from the kitchen to find out what all the excitement was about. William and Azura told her about the ship, and Madame Camus became excited for them. She said, "Then, if all you have to do is get along side and they will take you aboard. I assume that you plan to use a boat to approach the ship from the river."

William nodded, "Yes, Madame Camus, I plan to take one of the boats that you told me about. Now, we will have to wait until the night before they depart before we go to board the ship. Now they arrived late yesterday afternoon. When I saw the ship this morning, they had just begun to unload their cargo. Now, not counting today they will take three more days to unload their cargo, take on a new cargo, replenish their stores and fill their water casks. By then, it will be too late to leave that same day. No Captain wants to navigate the river at night, with those islands downstream. They will wait until the next morning at first light to get underway."

Madame Camus thought for a moment, then said, "Okay, this is Tuesday. You and Azura shall be taking a boat and going down river to board your uncle's ship Friday night."

William nodded. "Yes, Madame Camus, Azura and I shall board the ship Friday night. By then the moon will be setting shortly after eleven o-clock in the evening. Azura and I will leave here after it gets dark; and make our way to where the boats are tied up. We will then wait until the moon has set before we get out on the water. From there, it's not that far to the docks where the ships are tied up. Even though it will be dark, I'll be able to make out the ship. There is an inn across the road, just beyond where the ship is tied up. On a Friday night, there will be enough light coming from the inn for me to make out the outline of the ship."

Azura and Madame Camus could see that William had already come up with a plan. Azura, feeling delighted that they were to finally get away to America, said, "Oh, this is so wonderful, My Husband, I need to get our things ready to go, so that we shall be ready this Friday."

That evening at dinner, they talked more about what they had to do between now and Friday to be ready. William had decided that it was best that he not visit the docks in the vicinity of the Yankee Endeavor every day. Madame Camus and Azura had offered to go to the docks tomorrow in William's place. William could tell them just where along the docks the ship was moored and what to look for. William could then go again on Thursday. They could make the decision about Friday later.

The next day, William stayed at the house to do more work in the garden for Madame Camus. After doing the morning house cleaning, Madame Camus and Azura left to do the shopping. They went by way of the docks, coming out on the road near the docks close to the Yankee Endeavor. Azura was impressed by the size of the ship. They stopped at a wine shop near by to purchase two bottles of wine. From there, they went to the shops where they usually shopped to get the other things that they needed.

Arriving back home, Madame Camus and Azura told William of everything that they had observed near the ship. From their description of what they saw, he knew that the ship was still off-loading cargo. William figured that they would be finished off-loading cargo by that afternoon. They would then start loading a new cargo. Everything was going according to how William had imagined it would.

The next morning, after breakfast; Azura, with William's help, washed all their clothes that needed washing and hung them out to dry. After hanging out the wash to dry, Azura went shopping With Madame Camus. William stayed at the house to do some work for Madame Camus.

It was about three o-clock in the afternoon before William left for the docks. He took a route that put him across the road from the docks, up river from the Yankee Endeavor. After observing the activity on the docks, he walked down river to a sidewalk café where he could sit, with a glass of wine and observe the Yankee Endeavor; without being recognized by anyone aboard the ship. He made sure to make his observations seem casual, by continually shifting his focus to other activities along the docks. He could tell, by the state of taking on cargo and other activities about the ship, that they would still be there tomorrow.

That evening at dinner, they talked it over. It was decided that Madame Camus and Azura, after they did their shopping, would go to the docks on their way back home. All they had to do was check that the Yankee Endeavor was still there. William expected that the ship would still be there. He knew that if his Uncle Adam couldn't depart at or shortly after first light in the morning, he would wait until the next morning, wanting to be clear of the land before night fall.

William and Azura went to bed that evening knowing that this would be their last night in Madame Camus' home.

Friday morning after breakfast, William left to walk the route to where the boats were kept. He wanted to make sure that he had every house and street along the route down in his memory. He checked again where all the dogs were that would give an alarm. He didn't want to leave anything to chance.

Madame Camus and Azura departed for their shopping excursion, after they had completed the morning house cleaning. At the bakery madame Camus purchased bread. Azura purchased apricot tarts for dinner that evening. At the butcher shop, Azura purchased a pork loin to roast for dinner. They then shopped for brie and other things that Madame Camus needed.

After completing their shopping, they returned home; going by the docks to insure that the Yankee Endeavor was still there.

Dinner that evening was a little melancholy. William and Azura was excited at finally being able to leave for America; and at the same time, having to leave Madame Camus. In the time that they had been staying with her, they had become very close. Madame Camus also felt sad at seeing them go. At the same time, she felt that even though they were not really married, they really loved each other; and that it wouldn't be long before they made that commitment.

After dinner, they made sure that everything was packed. They left the bonnets rouge and the clothes that he had been wearing behind, no longer needing them. William and Azura had settled on a use for some of the coins that they had taken from the travel bag in the coach. Madame Camus should be really surprised to find the coins tied up in a handkerchief in their bedroom. Azura heated him some hot water to shave. She never grew tired of watching him shave. They then dressed in the darkest clothing they had. William dressed in Dark-blue cutaway coat, plumb color waistcoat and charcoal breeches. Azura wore her Indigo-blue gown and blue bonnet. She would keep her white lace fichu in her bag for now.

By the time they were ready, it was dark outside, With just a crescent moon for light. As they took their travel bags and Azura's hat box, Madame Camus was by the front Door. William said, "Good-bye, Madame Camus. You have really been such a big help for us. We Want to thank you."

Madame Camus said, "It was a pleasure to have you and Azura in my home. I wish you all the luck."

Azura then said, "Good-bye Madame Camus. I shall always remember the time we had together."

"And I shall always remember you, Mademoiselle Gauzet. Madame Camus said. She then whispered something in Azura's ear. Azura just nodded and smiled. Madame Camus held the door for them; and they stepped out into the night.

They looked up and down the road. There were hardly any people on the road. Most people were at home having dinner, or getting ready for bed. The only people about were those that were bound for, at an inn or tavern, or returning home. With the faint light from the crescent moon to guide them, they started up the road. They moved at a steady pace, that would get them to their destination in plenty of time; yet not so fast that they couldn't be alert for any threat.

They had gone almost a kilometer, when they heard a dog barking up ahead. They quickly took cover behind a hedge. Minutes later, two men, one carrying a lantern, turned a corner up ahead and passed by the hedge that they were hiding behind. William and Azura got a good look at them. They were members of the city night watch.

After the night watchmen were out of sight; William and Azura continued their journey. It took them almost an hour to reach the place where the boats were tied up. William first looked for the boat that he had decided to take. It was a small skiff, that was painted a dark-green. It would be very hard to see out on the river at night. After assuring that the boat was where he expected it to be. William and Azura found a place where they couldn't be observed. There they would wait until the moon went down.

At almost midnight, the moon dipped below the horizon. Now they could get to the boat, and get out into the river. William led Azura to the boat; and held it for her, as she got into the back of the boat. William then put the travel bags and hatbox in the boat in front of her. He then took a cord and tied it to where the boat was tied. The cord hung down into the water. At the end of the cord was a square of cloth, with some gold and silver coins wrapped in it and tied to the end of the cord. They were some of the coins that they had taken from the travel bag on the coach. William figured that if the boat was lost, the owner would be well compensated for it. He then got into the boat and sat between the oar locks. He then untied the boat, shoved it away from the dock and Fitted the oars in the locks

He mostly just let the boat drift down river on the current; using the oars just to keep it moving in the right direction and the proper distance from the river bank. Soon he could see the city docks ahead.

He was able to see the outline of the ships from the lights of the city behind them. As he neared where he thought where the Yankee Endeavor was tied up, he started to look for the lights of the inn that was across the road from it.

Finally, the form of the Yanked Endeavor materialized out of the darkness. William maneuvered the boat to drift down the side of the ship. About half way down he grabbed one of the fenders that were hung over the side when the ship was in port. After tying the boat to the top of the fender; William took his cane and rapped the but of the cane on the ships rail a couple of times. A few seconds later a voice called out, "Who's there?"

William recognized the voice. "Daniel Newbury, It's me, William Hooker."

Soon a head and pair of shoulders appeared above the rail. "William, what are you doing there this time of night?"

William said, "Just help us aboard. I'll explain it to you later. But first, are there any patrols near?"

Daniel replied, "You know that patrolling at night is thirsty work. They are at the inn wetting their throats."

With a little chuckle, William said, "Good."

William first handed their bags and hat box up. He and Daniel then helped Azura up onto the ship. Last, William started to climb up, using the rope that the fender was suspended from. As he did so, he untied the boat and shoved it with his foot to drift out into the middle of the river.

Once everyone was aboard. Daniel led them down below decks to the Captain's Cabin. There, Daniel knocked on the door. A voice, grumpy from being awakened from sleep, called out, "What do you want!"

Daniel called out, "Captain Hooker, Sir, your nephew William is here with his lady."

A minute later the door opened. Captain Hooker stood there in a robe and slippers. "William, how did you get here at this unlikely hour?" William was about to say something, when his uncle waved his hand. "Save it for tomorrow, William, I need my sleep. Daniel, put them in the passenger cabin."

William's uncle closed the door to get back to bed. Daniel led them to a door a few steps away. He opened the door to the passenger cabin. Taking a small taper from a small cup attached to the wall, he lit it from the flame of his lantern; then used it to light a lamp that was attached to the wall. "Okay," Daniel said, "This is your and your misses' cabin. Have a good night."

As soon as the door was closed. William and Azura looked around the cabin. It was small. There was a bed that two people could sleep in, a small locker to hang clothes in, a small table attached to the wall and two chairs attached to the deck.

Until this moment, they hadn't realized just how exhausted they were. It wasn't just from the night walk, the trip down river by boat, or the late hour. It was also the anxiety of it all. They didn't even take the time to undress for bed. William just removed his cutaway coat, waistcoat, cravat and shoes. Azura removed only her gown and shoes. They turned out the lamp and got into bed. They were both in a deep sleep in a few minutes.

SEVENTEEN

It was mid-morning by the time William and Azura awoke. As usual, Azura was the first to awaken. There was a moment of disorientation as to her whereabouts, then she recalled being shone to the cabin on the ship. She quickly got up and started to put on her gown. As she was fastening her gown, William started to stir. His eyes opened, and he looked at Azura.

Azura smiled at him. "Good-morning, My Husband."

With a nod, William responded, "Good-morning, My Wife."

He quickly got out of bed and started to dress. As he dressed, he looked at Azura. "We are on my Uncle's ship now and no longer in jeopardy. You need not address me as, My Husband. You may just address me as William; and I shall address you as Azura, if you like."

Looking at him, Azura replied, "But I have grown accustomed to addressing you as, My Husband, I wish to continue to do so for now."

William gave it a moments thought, then said, "Then, My Wife, you may continue to do so for now."

Once they were both dressed, William said, "Are you hungry, My Wife? I'm sure that the crew had breakfast before we left port this morning. However, if we go to the galley, I'm sure that the cook can fix us something."

Azura nodded. "Yes, My Husband, let's go to the galley and see what the cook can do for us."

William led the way to the galley. There they found the cook starting to prepare for the next meal. William knew the cook. "Hay, Roger, we missed breakfast this morning. Do you have something for us?"

Roger looked to see William and Azura. He had heard, as the rest of the crew had, about how William and his wife Monique, had come aboard in the middle of the night. "Okay, William, I can help you and the misses. How about bacon and eggs? I also have some left-over biscuits from breakfast. If that's all right with you?"

"That will be just fine." William said.

It was only a few minutes before the cook had breakfast for them. They quickly had breakfast; then returned to their cabin. With his uncle Adam and crew busy handling the ship down the narrow river channel; he didn't feel that they should go up on deck until they were in the estuary. By then, William's uncle Adam would have time for them. They didn't mind staying in their cabin for now. Even though they had gotten a good night's sleep, they were still weary from their ordeal.

Two hours later the ship was in the estuary. Captain Hooker turned the quarterdeck over to his first mate, Brook Townley. He then went down below to see William and Monique.

There was a knock at the door. William opened the door to see his Uncle Adam. "Come in, Uncle Adam."

Captain Hooker entered the cabin, closing the door behind himself. "Well, William, now you can tell me, why you and Monique had to come aboard by stealth in the middle of the night."

William cleared his throat. He knew that it was going to be a long explanation. "Well, Uncle Adam, It's like this. First, this is not Monique. She is Mademoiselle Azura Gauzet."

His uncle said, "Not Monique! Then what about Monique?"

William Continued, "I guess that you left Newport before the letter arrived from Monique's father. Well, about five weeks before I arrived in Reims, Monique fell ill from tetanus and died. After spending a few days with her family; I started back home,

"I stopped over in Paris for the night and took a room. I couldn't sleep, so I went for a walk. As I was walking down the street, I heard a woman scream. I rushed to the alleyway from where the scream was coming from. There, Azura was being assaulted by two men. I immediately went to her assistance. Well, when it was over, the two men lay dead on the pavement. After hiding the bodies; I took Azura back to my room. There I found out that she had been in the service of Contessa Marie Jeanne Du Barry; and the Committee of Public Safety was looking for her. For both mine and her safety, I had to take her with me. The only way I could do that was to have her pose as my wife Monique, so that she could use Monique's travel documents. That Is why we had to come aboard in the middle of the night. They were looking for us."

William's uncle nodded. "Well, I guess that explains the patrols on the docks in Bordeaux."

William nodded. "Yes, Uncle Adam, they were looking for us."

William now turned to Azura. "Well, Azura, Uncle Adam knows about us now. You are safe now. We need no longer to share a bed. You can have the cabin for yourself. I shall sleep up forward with the crew."

With a cry, Azura grabbed William's arm with both arms. "But I want you in my bed. You gave me your solemn oath that you would defend my virtue as well as my person, that you would never abandon me and that as long as I was with you no harm would come to me. You have kept your oath; you have earned the right to share my bed."

William looked into Azura's eyes for a few seconds. He then turned to his uncle. "Uncle Adam, you are the Captain of the Yankee Endeavor, and we are now at sea. I want you to marry us right now."

Azura let out a squeal of delight, as she wrapped both arms about William's neck and started kissing him on the face and lips.

Captain Hooker stifled a chuckle. "I take it that you want to Marry William."

"Yes, Oh, Yes! I want to marry William!" Azura exclaimed.

Captain Hooker said, "Then I shall get my bible, then meet you on deck when you are ready." He then left the cabin, closing the door behind him.

As soon as the door closed, William turned to Azura. She was wearing her indigo-blue gown. He said, "Azura, why don't you change into one of the gowns that I gave you in Paris? They are quite good gowns for such an event as our wedding."

Azura shook her head. "No, William, I can't do that. True they are splendid gowns, much better that any I have ever owned. However, they first belonged to Monique, then to your sister, Tandra. When I marry, I want to be in my own gown. The one I have on now will do quite well. I will, however, wear the hat that you gave me. Being the first gift from you, it means a lot to me."

Azura took her lace fichu from her travel bag and put it on. She then took her hat from the hat box and placed it on her head. "I am ready, William."

Before they left the cabin, William went over with her the words that they would say in the wedding ceremony; especially the words that they would say during the exchange of rings. He then took his and the ring that he had given her in Paris to wear. William then led Azura up on deck.

Captain Hooker was waiting for them on the quarterdeck. Mounting the steps to the quarterdeck, Captain Hooker had William and Azura stand, with Azura to William's left, at the forward rail, with their backs to the main deck, where the crew had been assembled. Captain Hooker opened his bible. William placed the rings in the fold of the bible. They were now ready.

Captain Hooker now said in a strong voice that carried the full length of the ship. "Gentlemen, we are assembled her to witness the joining of William Hooker and Azura Gauzet in the bonds of matrimony. William Hooker, Azura Gauzet, are you ready to take your vows?"

Both William and Azura responded, "Yes."

Captain Hooker looked first at Azura. "Azura Gauzet, will you take William Hooker to be your wedded husband. To have and to hold from this day forward for better, or for worst, for richer, for poorer, in sickness and in health, to love and to cherish till death do you part, according to God's holy law."

Azura responded, "I will."

Captain Hooker then looked at William. "William Hooker, will you take Azura Gauzet as your wedded wife. To have and to hold from this day forward for better, or for worst, for richer, for poorer, in sickness and in health, to love and to cherish till death do you part, according to Gods holy law."

William responded, "I will."

Captain Hooker then took the ring for William and handed it to Azura. As Azura placed the ring on the ring finger of William's left hand, she said, "I give you this ring as a symbol of my devotion to you. With this ring I thee wed."

Captain Hooker then took the ring for Azura and handed it to William. As William placed the ring on the ring finger of Azura's left hand, he said, "I give you this ring as a symbol of my devotion to you. With this ring I thee wed."

Captain Hooker then said, "I now declare you husband and wife. William, you may now kiss your bride."

As William enfolded Azura in his arms and kissed her, a cheer went up from the crew.

Captain Hooker now said, "It shall be entered into the ship's log, that on this day at this time William Hooker and Azura Gauzet entered into the bonds of matrimony, Captain Adam Hooker officiating, witnessed by first mate Brook Townley and the crew of the Yankee Endeavor. Now, crew dismissed from quarters."

As the crew went about their duties, Captain Hooker kissed Azura on the cheek. "Welcome to the family, Mrs. Azura Hooker. I would be pleased that you call me, Uncle Adam."

Azura was at the pinnacle of happiness. Events had moved so fast that she could hardly believe it. She was William's wife for real now, not just a pretend bride; and Uncle Adam was welcoming her into the family. Returning the kiss to the cheek, Azura said, "Thank you, Uncle Adam."

The ship's cook threw himself into his work. The evening meal had to be something special in honor of William and Azura's wedding. Having just left port, he had an abundance of fresh stores. Working all afternoon, by the evening meal, he had baked a cake. He also had roast beef, potatoes, fresh vegetables and rolls. There was even wine for the crew to drink a toast to the bride and groom. The whole affair became very festive.

That evening in their cabin, William finally asked her about what had been on his mind since they left Madame Camus' home. "Azura, what did Madame Camus whisper in your ear, as we were leaving her home?"

Azura shrugged. "Oh, not much. She just told me that all you needed was a little push, for you to ask me to marry you."

William didn't have to say anything more. He now wondered about her grabbing his arm. How much was purely spontaneous, and how much planned.

William and Azura got ready for bed. This time they both disrobed together. Each looking forward to this night that they had thought about for quite a while.

When Azura was disrobed, the last thing that she removed was the cloth money belt that she had worn, ever since her mother had tied it about her waist. Presenting it to William, she said, "My Husband, this is the money that my mother gave me. It was to have been my dowry. It is now yours."

William accepted the dowry, knowing it the proper thing to do. "Thank you, My Wife, we shall both find some use for it."

When they were ready, William turned the lamp down, and they got into bed. That night they consummated their marriage.

Three days out from Bordeaux, they spotted a British Royal Navy Ship. It was far off and they had the advantage of the wind, so the British ship didn't even attempt to challenge them.

The Yankee Endeavor sailed west until they were clear of the Iberian Peninsula, then turned southwest to the Azores. Near the Azores, they turned west to let the westerly trade winds carry them across the Atlantic Ocean.

Before turning north for home, Captain Hooker made a port call at Havana, Cuba. There He was able to sell some of the wine from Bordeaux at a good profit. He then took on a cargo of rum, cane sugar, cane syrup and Cuban cigars. In his bargaining with the Spanish import exporters, Captain Hooker found Azura's fluency in Spanish very useful.

While in Havana, William and Azura had some time to look about the city. They found it to be a very exotic place. More so than any other city they had ever visited.

From Havana, they sailed north, taking advantage of the gulf stream to help carry them north. They had good winds and made good time.

Finally, just before noon of a lovely fall day, they came in sight of land. Soon they could see Newport, Rhode Island in the brilliance of the noon-day sun. They were home. Now they would face William's Family. He had gone to France for Monique. Now he was returning with Azura. He would have to explain it to them.

EIGHTEEN

It was mid afternoon, when the last line was made secure, and the Yankee Endeavor rested at the dock at Newport, Rhode Island. William Hooker and his Wife Azura were below decks in the Captain's cabin, as requested by the Captain, their Uncle Adam.

William's father, James, had been notified of the approach of the Yankee Endeavor, and was on the dock to meet it. Looking to the quarterdeck, He saw his brother, Captain Adam Hooker, standing next to the barnacle. As soon as the gangplank was run out and secured, James went aboard to see his brother.

Captain Hooker, having seen his brother, had descended from the quarterdeck to the main deck to meet his brother. As they shook hands, James said, "Welcome home, Adam. How was your trip?"

Captain Hooker responded, "It was a very good trip. We couldn't get in at Nantes, so we put in at Bordeaux. At Bordeaux we took on some fine Bordeaux wines, also some silks and other fine cloth and other things. On the way back, we stopped off at Havana. There we sold some of the wine at a good profit. We then took on rum, cane sugar, cane Syrup and Cuban cigars."

James nodded. "Yes, it does sound like you had a good trip."

Captain Hooker said, "James, there is something else that I need to speak to you about. Why don't you come down to my cabin?"

"Why, yes, of course." James said.

James followed his brother down to the captain's cabin. When they got there, Adam opened the door and let his brother enter first. Entering the Captain's cabin. James saw his son, William, standing there. There was also a young lady that he didn't know standing next to him.

"Hello, Father." William said.

William's father embraced him, saying, "Hello, William."

Before anything else could be said, William took Azura by the hand. "Father, I have someone to introduce to you. This is Mrs. Azura Hooker, My wife."

William's father didn't say anything for several seconds. He just stood there, looking back and forth from William to Azura. Finally, he said, "How did this happen?"

William said, "Well, Father, it's a long story."

James brother then said, "Perhaps we can have a seat; and William and Azura can tell you about it."

The captain's cabin was spacious enough. There was an upholstered bench seat running across the back of the cabin, under the stern windows. There was also a small table and two chairs bolted to the deck. As soon as everyone was seated. Adam poured a glass of wine for everyone.

William then started to tell the story, with a contribution from time to time from Azura. William told of how he had arrived at Reims to find that Monique had died. Of how he had started back home, stopping in Paris for a night's lay over. Then how he had come to the rescue of Azura. He then told his father of how he had concluded that his and Azura's destinies were intertwined, that to insure his own safety, he had to look to hers also. He then told about the trip across France to Bordeaux. Then finally getting aboard Uncle Adan's ship in the middle of the night.

When he had finished, his father said, "I say, William, that's quite some story."

William's father now turned to Azura. "If everything William said about you is true, then you must be an exceptional young woman. Embracing her, he said, "Welcome to the family, Azura. You may address me as, father."

Azura's heart leap with relief and happiness, as she fought to hold back tears of joy; she had been accepted by William's father. She was now sure that she would be welcomed by the rest of the family. "Thank you, Father."

William's father now said, "I have to get back to the store. William, why don't you and Azura go on home. I'm sure that your mother will be surprised and glad to see you and Azura."

As William and Azura walked through Newport, Azura kept looking around at what was now her new home. Newport was much larger than the hamlet in France where she had grown up. It was a true city, but much smaller than the cities of France. It was no bigger than a neighborhood in Versailles. It would certainly be lost in a city the size of Paris. Even so, she found it to be a lovely place to call home. She felt an energy pulsing through the city that she had never felt anywhere in France. This was a place that was young and growing. She just knew that she would love it here.

They came to a large house near the edge of the city. William said, "This is my Parent's home; the house that I grew up in."

He didn't even bother to knock, but just opened the door and stepped in with Azura. "Mom, I'm home!"

A few seconds later, William's mother came out from the door to the kitchen next to the stair. Rushing to embrace William, she cried out. "Oh, William, I'm so happy to have you home."

After hugging William and kissing him on the cheek, his mother said. Who is this young lady with you, William?"

William put his arm about Azura's waist. Azura was really nervous, in anticipation of meeting William's mother. "Mom, this is Azura, your daughter-in-law. Azura, this is my mother."

William's mother was taken completely by surprise, but quickly recovered. She needed to know about this young woman that William had brought home. However, she would leave that for later. She embraced Azura, kissing her on the cheeks. "Welcome, Azura. Let us go into the kitchen, where we can be comfortable."

In the kitchen, William's mother had William and Azura take a seat at the kitchen table. "I'm sure that you are hungry. I have some fresh apple pies in the pie safe and fresh milk."

William nodded. "That will be fine, Mom."

William's mother cut William and Azura a slice of apple pie, then served it with glasses of milk. She then had a seat at the table with them. "Now, William, you can tell me about Azura."

It was a long story, and the pie and milk were finished long before it was finished. William's mother just sat for the most of it listening, only occasionally asking a question. When William and Azura had finish, William's mother had gotten to know a lot about Azura. She had begun to see why her son had taken to Azura. She seemed to be a very exceptionable young woman. Finally, William's mother hugged

Azura, saying, "Welcome to the family, my Daughter. Just call me mother, or mom."

Now Azura could no longer hold back the tears of joy. "Oh, thank you, Mother." She knew that with William's mother's approval, everyone else would welcome her.

Later, when William's brother's and sister's arrived home from school; Azura, along with William was there to greet them. Their mother made the introduction of Azura to her children. The younger one's were thrilled to have a new sister. William's brother, Samuel, thought that Azura, with her stunning blue eyes and fine-pale blonde hair was an exceptionally beautiful young woman. Tandra, encountering a young woman of her own age, wanted to get to know her better.

After the introductions, William took Azura up to his room in his parent's home, where they would stay for a few more days, until their house was ready. The first thing that Azura noticed was Monique's portrait on the wall, over William's bed. She knew of Monique, but hadn't known what she had looked like until now. She had to admit that she had been an attractive young woman.

Seeing Azura looking at Monique's portrait. William said, "That was Monique. I shall have to take it up to the attic for storage."

Azura said, "You don't have to do it right away. I know that she meant a lot to you."

After putting their clothing away in the armoire, they got ready for dinner. Azura had been wearing her indigo-blue gown for a long time. She changed into the only other gown that she had. It was a plain, but well made of a good quality linen of jade-green.

At dinner that evening, William and Azura entertained the family with more accounts of their adventures in France. They were especially moved by their account of how they had been able to get aboard the Yankee Endeavor in the middle of the night.

After dinner, William went up to their room to get the bundle that contained the gowns that Monique's mother had given him, to give to his sister, Tandra. Giving the gowns to Tandra, William told her how Azura had used them during their flight across France by coach.

Tandra opened the bundle. The gowns were indeed beautiful, and of good quality. She then looked at what Azura was wearing. She knew that Azura had little clothing with her; and nothing equal to these gowns. Tandra knew what she had to do. Holding out the bundle of gowns, she said. "Azura, I have no other wedding gift for you. It would please me if you would accept these gowns as my gift to you."

Azura was moved by Tandra's generosity. "Thank you, Tandra; I shall think of you whenever I wear them."

Tandra knew then that she would love to have Azura as her sister-in-law.

That night in bed, Azura felt secure for the first time since leaving home. She now knew that she was where she belonged.

The next day, Willian went back to work. Azura kept busy helping her Mother-in-law with the house cleaning and cooking. She was enjoying the time spent with her mother-in-law. It was bringing them closer together.

Sunday, Azura went to church with the rest of the family. There she was introduced to many friends of the family. She couldn't remember everyone's names all at once. She would just have to get to know them more later on.

After church, the family went back home. Sunday was a time of leisure for everyone. Azure and Tandra helped their mother cook the evening meal. For Dinner, William's brother, Thomas and his family came over for dinner. Azura felt secure in being a member of such a large and loving family.

She thought of her mother back in France. She was alone now, all her daughter's having their own families. If she could, Azura would like to have her mother join her and William here in America. She felt that her mother would really love to be here.

Finally, on Tuesday evening, as they were getting ready for bed, William said, Well, My Wife, everything is ready. Tomorrow you shall see your new home. After breakfast, we shall Pack our bags. Then I shall hitch up our gig. Then we shall leave for our new home." Azura hugged and kissed him. "Oh, My Husband, I can hardly wait to see our new home."

That night, even after making love with William; Azura was still so excited that she found it hard to get to sleep.

The next morning, after breakfast, they packed their bags, hitched up their gig and set out for their new home. They only had about two and one-half miles to go, so they were there in less than thirty minutes. When William pulled into the drive, and Azura became aware that this was their house, she was amazed at how large it was. It was easily five or six times the size of her mother's house in France. "This is our house, My Husband? It's so big. It's almost as big as a chateau in France. What shall we do with all the room?'

William laughed at her amazement. "Well, My Wife, we shall fill it with happy children."

She looked at him. "You mean, that I will fill it with happy children."

William then laughed again, and Azura laughed with him.

Azura's last time of the moon came and went, without the expected outcome. In six more day's her time of the moon would come again. If nothing happened, then she would know for sure that she was with child. Till then it would be her secret.

William stopped the gig at the front door. He then helped Azura down, then took their baggage. He opened the front door, then turned to Azura. The Roman's had a superstition, that if a bride tripped on the threshold the first time, she entered her new home, there would be bad luck. To guard against this, the husband carried her over the threshold." He then picked her up in his arms and carried her over the threshold.

As he lowered her feet to the floor, Azura got her first look at the inside of hers and William's house. It was just as grand on the inside as it was on the outside. There was a wide hallway running from the front door to the stairs at the back of the house, with doors to two rooms to each side of the house.

William pointed. "There is a door to the kitchen on the left, just before the stairs. You can also go through the dining room, that's the second door to the left, then to the kitchen. The second floor has the same arrangement of rooms. There is plenty of storage space in the attic. There is also a large root cellar at the back of the house, the other side of the stairs from the kitchen. Now, you can have a look around, while I put away the gig.

William left her in the house, as he went back outside to put the gig in the barn. William was back a few minutes later. He then showed Azura the whole house. There were furnishings for the sitting room,

Dining room and four bed rooms. That left two rooms on the first floor for other uses. William had decided that one would make a good office. The other, he hadn't yet decided what to do with.

Azura loved the kitchen. It was more than twice the size of her mother's kitchen. There was a cast iron stove and oven, a large kitchen table, pie safe, cabinets, all the pots and pans and cooking utensils needed. There was even a large pantry that had been stocked.

Azura turned to William. "Oh, My Husband, I love it. This is what every woman dreams of having. If it is a dream, I hope that I never wake-up."

William laughed. Tis no dream, My Wife; it all yours, you are the mistress of this house."

Azura fell into his arms and kissed him with passion.

William then said. Let us go outside so that I can show you all the rest. Leaving through the outside door to the kitchen; William took her first to the barn. He showed her the large space at the front of the barn, where the gig was kept. He pointed out the tool room, feed room, tack room and milking stalls. When they came to the horse stalls, there were two horses in the stalls. One was the one that had pulled the gig. William pointed to the other. "This, My Wife, is your horse. I also have a side saddle and the rest of the tack for you. Have you ever ridden a horse?"

Azura shook her head. "No, My Husband, in France only the aristocracy ride horses, the common people walk."

William smiled at her. "Well, My Wife, I shall teach you to ride as a proper lady. I'm sure that you shall love it. Her name is Ginger. She is a gentle creature and will be just right for you.

William then took her outside to show her the rest of the property.

When at last he had shown her everything, he said, "Well, My Wife, why don't we go in and make this house a home?"

She replied, "Yes, My Husband, let us do that."

EPILOGUE

T en days after they moved into their new home, Azura was certain that she was pregnant. William was delighted with the news. They both then told William's parents, who were also thrilled at the news. William's mother wasted no time in advising Azura in her pregnancy and coming birth.

From the day that William had arrived back home with Azura; his parents had started to plan for a church wedding. Eighteen days after William and Azura moved into their home, they had the wedding in the church. All of William's family and friends attended. The wedding and reception were the family social event of the year.

Azura wrote to her mother about making it to Paris. Of how William rescued her; and their trip across France to Bordeaux. Finally, she told her mother about taking the ship to America. She told her mother about her life in America and their home. She told her mother that if she wanted to come to America to live with them, that they already had a bedroom ready for her. Last she told her mother that she was going to make her a Grandmother again.

A month after William and Azura had gotten away from Bordeaux; Monsieur Proust was recalled by the Paris Committee of Public Safety. Monsieur Proust regretted returning to Paris without having succeeded in capturing his pray. He also didn't look forward to the reception that he would get upon his return to Paris.

On the 8th of December 1793, Madame Marie Jeanne Du Barry was executed by beheading. On the way to the guillotine, she collapsed in the cart that she was being carried in and cried, "You are going to hurt me! Why?" Terrified, she screamed to the crowd that was there to watch the execution for mercy and begged them for help. Her last words to the executioner, so it is said, were << De grace, Monsieur le bourreau, encore un petit moment>> "One Moment, Mr. Executioner, I beg you."

It was not only the nobility that suffered beheading by the guillotine. Countless common people also went to the guillotine; in most cases their only crime being that they had been in service to, are were associated with the aristocracy. There was, however, one young woman, Mademoiselle Azura Gauzet, who escaped the guillotine; she was never found.

Early in 1794, Madame Gauzet decided to join her daughter in America. She left her house in France to her three other daughters. Taking ship, she arrived in Newport, Rhode Island in time to witness the birth of her Grandson.

Printed in the United States
By Bookmasters